The Fae Ring

Book Two

Highland Secrets Trilogy

THE FAE RING

HIGHLAND SECRETS

book two

by

C.A. SZAREK

other books by c.a. szarek

<u>Highland Secrets Trilogy & Companions</u>—<u>Historical Fantasy Romance</u>
The Princess and The Laird (Highland Secrets Prequel)
The Tartan MP3 Player (Book One)
The Fae Ring (Book Two)
The Parchment Scroll (Book Three)
Highland Valentine (A Highland Secrets HEA Story)
Highlander's Portrait (A Highland Secrets Story)

<u>Highland Treasures</u>—<u>Historical Fantasy Romance</u>
Highland Oath (Book One)
Highland Essence (Book Two)
Highland Skies (Book Three)

<u>The King's Riders</u>—<u>Fantasy Romance</u>
Sword's Call (Book One)—*Also in Audio*
Love's Call (Book Two)—*Also in Audio*
Rogue's Call (Book Three)—*Also in Audio*
Fate's Call (A Novella from the World of the King's Riders)—*Also in Audio*

<u>Crossing Forces</u>—<u>Romantic Suspense</u>

Collision Force (Book One) — *Also in Audio*

Cole in Her Stocking (A Crossing Forces Christmas) — *FREE read!*

Chance Collision (Book Two) — *Also in Audio*

Calculated Collision (Book Three) — *Also in Audio*

Collision Control (Book Four) — *Also in Audio*

Weekend Collision (A Crossing Forces HEA Story) — *FREE read!*

Superior Collision (Book Five) — *Also in Audio*

Incendiary Collision (Book Six) — *Coming Soon!*

<u>The Giovanni</u>

King of Hearts (Book One) — *Also in Audio*

Queen of Diamonds (Book Two) — *Coming Soon!*

Dedication

For my husband, Shane. Even though this one doesn't have cops and robbers. I write because I am, and I love you even more for understanding.

chapter one

The waves crashed over the rocks with violence, but that was fine with Janet.

It fit her mood perfectly.

Frigid air buffeted the MacLeod plaid around her shoulders, but she didn't hold it tighter to protect herself from the gooseflesh that rose on her bare forearms and the back of her neck. Her hair flew in her eyes. She ignored that bother, too.

Shivers from the bite in the air chased each other down her spine, but Janet didn't care if she froze. She'd regret it later, most likely.

"Ye'll catch yer death," many an older MacLeod would scold. She could see the concern in their eyes.

"Jesu," Janet muttered. She smirked. If anyone overheard her cursing like a man, she would be admonished for sure.

If one more person asked her, *"Are ye well, lass?"* she was going to scream.

Or…hit someone.

Violence was much more Alex and Duncan than it ever had been Janet, but…

Her brothers might be her first and second victims.

They were driving her crazy with their concern, as

much as with their open affection for the women they loved.

Their wives…Janet loved them. She really did.

However, both were expecting.

How am I supposed to handle that?

Where was her place?

How — *where* — did she fit in?

She wanted to shout to the whole clan; father, brothers, cousins, even MacLeods that weren't direct blood — *"Leave me be, I'm well, hale, braw!"*

But am I?

Her father had never married her off. Suitors hadn't knocked down the doors, either.

From the time her mother had gotten sick, Janet had run Dunvegan. She'd been three and ten, and the twins twenty.

Then their mother had passed. Janet had been barely six and ten.

She'd instantly been made the Lady of the castle, and the clan.

Her father had never remarried, and nor would he. Janet's duties had continued even when her brother Alex — elder of the twins — had assumed the role of laird a few years ago when their father had stepped down to care for their mother when she had ailed most severely.

Now Alex had his lovely Fae princess wife — Alana. They'd married ten years before in secret, but she was finally in the Human Realm with her man and young lad, Angus. Now their second bairn was on the way.

Alana hadn't been living at Dunvegan for very long. Although, it was no wonder the couple was expecting. They weren't shy about their love for each other. Everyone teased her laird brother that he couldn't keep his hands off his bonnie wife. They'd lived apart for years, their relationship hidden to all except Janet, Duncan, and their father so the public kisses in corridors were no surprise.

A year ago, the King of the Fae, Alana's father, had kidnapped Alex when he'd discovered his daughter had married a human. Janet's brother had been starved and held hostage for six months. Alana, too, had been a captive in her own palace, locked in the tower.

Duncan, the younger twin, had scoured the lands and the sea—not to mention all the islands of the Hebrides—to find the Faery Stones, the magical gateway into the Realm of the Fae.

Magic.

Janet shook her head.

Before Alex's confession about Alana, right before their son was born, Janet had never believed in faeries. Just old Scottish legends.

Although it was Clan MacLeod lore that the blood of the Fae ran through their veins. Six hundred years before, a Fae princess had married the laird.

Her father swore by the tale.

She'd never believed.

If she'd not seen her nephew work magic, she still might not. Angus, who was almost ten, had lived with them at Dunvegan his entire life.

Janet had raised the lad from the time he was a few hours old. She'd actually helped bring her nephew into the world. She was close to the lad, and didn't regret caring for him, but she'd made sure he knew she was not his mother.

That smarted a bit.

She didn't want to claim him for her own, but she very much wanted a child. Janet also wanted a man to look at her the way Alex looked at Alana, and Duncan looked at Claire.

Bairns. We'll have two.

Claire was also expecting. Their first child would be here in less than three months, before Alex and Alana's. She'd only been with them for six months, but she was already a MacLeod. Everyone loved her. She was family, as much as Duncan or Alex was to Janet.

Family.

Janet had it in spades.

She loved them, but her heart ached with envy.

Guilt rushed up from her stomach because her feelings weren't right. Janet couldn't justify ill notions no matter how hard she tried.

That just made her feel worse.

She didn't have a husband. Or a bairn on the way.

At six and twenty, what man would want her now?

Even though she still had her virtue, Janet wasn't a pink-cheeked innocent little lass with stars in her eyes. She'd never been tiny or petite like Alana or Claire. She was too tall, too broad-shouldered. Wide-hipped.

Janet sighed.

Water crashed against the rocks, stirring the cold air around her even more.

Awareness of someone's eyes on her prickled down her spine.

She glanced over her shoulder, but he wasn't facing her.

Xander was looking toward Dunvegan, the stronghold of her clan. He held his broad shoulders tight, his back straight despite the fact one of his knees was bent, perched on a boulder.

The former Fae Warrior was kin to Alex's wife, and he'd been living in the Human Realm since Alana had fled her father. He was the princess' bodyguard, and he swore to protect her for life.

He could read minds; Janet had been told. So, he spent much time alone.

The Fae man had to be the most handsome she'd ever seen. His hair was so pale blond it was almost silver. Eyes that were deeply hued, more violet than blue. Xander was tall, perhaps an inch or so more than her brothers.

When he'd made the decision to live with humans, he'd cut his braid off, or so Alana had explained. He was no longer a Fae Warrior, but anyone who looked at him could see he was built to fight. Xander was also missing his wings, because there was less magic in the Human Realm, according to her sister-by-marriage.

Janet couldn't imagine a person who could fly, like an angel, but it would probably make him even more handsome.

Alana had said his wings were a huge part of her cousin, and their absence greatly contributed to his melancholy. She was worried about him; she'd voiced on several occasions.

Janet had rarely seen him smile.

The wind shifted his short locks. Xander's expression was hard, and he exuded dark emotions.

She stared, studying his strong profile. Janet couldn't tear her eyes away.

Even obviously sorrowful, he was beautiful, especially standing up on the ridge like that. Her heart missed a beat.

Perhaps Xander was as lost as she.

He still didn't look her way.

It's for the better.

I cannot help myself, let alone another.

Janet sighed and turned back to the rough waters.

chapter two

Xander watched her from a distance; concerned she was too cold, but Lady Janet stared into the crashing waves without notice of anything else—including his presence on the rocky outcropping above her.

The sea was as stormy as her expression this morning.

He adjusted the sword at his waist and rested his booted foot on a boulder. He couldn't tear his eyes from the lass. Didn't need his cousin Alana's empathic magic to know how Lady Janet was feeling.

Why?

The sister to the Laird MacLeod—his cousin's husband—was usually jovial. Rarely seen without a smile. Lady Janet was take-charge and strong, as well as beautiful. Her dark hair only made her sapphire eyes more obvious.

Instinct told him to go to her. Make her smile.

Odd. Where's that coming from?

Xander squared his shoulders and shook his head, turning toward the great castle looming in the distance behind him.

Nothing was amiss at Dunvegan.

His current location prevented him from hearing the clash of swords, but the MacLeods were training in the bailey. He'd watched for a while, but Duncan and Alex MacLeod had their men under control, instructing, sparring, and taking bets as men did.

Xander clenched his jaw. He'd sworn to protect Alana for life. He and the princess—*former* princess now—had been linked.

His cousin was finally happy with the man she loved, as well as her little lad. She was the laird's wife, Lady MacLeod of Dunvegan.

Where was *his* place here?

She didn't need his fighting skills. Her husband was strong—physically as well as in his position as laird. He had plenty of men—kinsmen and men-at-arms—to defend his family and castle.

Not to mention the laird's twin brother, Duncan. The man acted as Alex's second in everything. Captained the men who fought for them as well, as War Chief.

Besides, without Xander's wings and with his diminished magic, what good was he?

Awareness washed over him, and he glanced back down to the beach. Lady Janet still studied the crashing waters in the bitter chill, but she'd been looking at him. His gut told him so, even if she was not at the moment.

He watched her skirts whip around her legs. The plaid around her slipped from one shoulder, but she made no move to grab and wrap it around herself.

Xander frowned. If it weren't Lady Janet before him, he would've been able to pick up her thoughts. For some reason, she was the only human he couldn't read. Mind reading was his only magic that wasn't affected in the Human Realm.

Unfortunately.

Humans didn't have the ability to consciously hide their thoughts, so the conversations in his head were constant.

Torture.

Spending time with Alana and Angus was the only peace he had. His cousin helped center him and could cast a spell to help him deal with it, but Xander wouldn't ask that of her again. He'd needed her magic for the first few weeks in the Human Realm, but no more.

He was strong. Needed to adapt.

Xander's lot in life had been chosen from the moment he'd accompanied Alana. He'd cut his warrior braid and sealed his fate.

He'd remain with humans for the rest of his long life.

Fae were not immortal, but they lived two—sometimes even three—times longer than humans.

It wasn't known if being away from the Fae Realm for an extended period of time would change that.

He was more than his magic, he knew that well, but he couldn't help but envy his cousin and her lad. Alana's royal blood gifted her with powers he couldn't even fathom. Her magic was varied and concentrated, and not affected very much in this realm. Angus, being half human, had less than his mother, but every day he was coming into his powers more.

Xander had been a fool to take magic for granted.

When the wind carried what sounded like a sob to his ears, he locked his gaze onto Lady Janet.

The lass is crying?

He startled when his wings didn't respond, destroying his intention to glide down to the beach. His spine tingled and no magic responded.

Goddess, you should be used to that by now.

Xander shook his head.

It doesn't matter.

He wanted — no, *needed* — to make Lady Janet feel better.

Xander didn't question the urge.

His jump down to the rocks and sand wasn't with as much finesse as he would've liked, but he felt her gaze before he met it.

She didn't smile, and for some reason, his heart stuttered.

He needed to see the curve of her full mouth.

Why?

Despite living in the same place for the past six months, he didn't know her well — hardly at all, in fact. She was sister-by-marriage to his cousin, and a lady.

Xander had kept an appropriate distance. As he would have from a Fae of her station had he still been home. His rank amongst the Warriors had been high, but still not the same class as a noble. His mother had been a princess—until she'd married his father, the *winged* captain of the King's Royal Guard.

His father, Daegus, had his own prestige of course, but King Fillan had not wanted him as a match for his sister. They'd married in secret and bound themselves in magic as well as love. It couldn't have been torn asunder without either—or both—of their deaths.

Because of his value to King Fillan, Xander's father had been forgiven—eventually.

His mother never was.

The king did not consider him nephew, only Warrior, and had used him as such.

Alana had never obeyed her father and had always kept Xander close. As children, caretakers gave up on trying to keep them apart. The princess wouldn't mind governess or magic tutors. The queen had never fought to separate them, so Xander had been permitted the same lessons as Alana.

Childhood memories flitted through his head.

Home had changed.

Home was now the Human Realm.

Home was with the MacLeods.

Don't think of what is lost.

Lady Janet was no longer looking his way as he approached.

Xander lifted the plaid that'd slipped off her shoulder and wrapped her in it. He watched his hand as if it were not his own. He'd never reached out to her before.

Big blue eyes met his gaze, and she wiped her cheeks. "Thank ye, Sir Xander, but that dinnae be necessary." Her voice was thick and laced with sadness.

His stomach fluttered but he forced a shake of his head. "I don't want you to get cold, lass." The address was technically inappropriate, because she was a lady, but he couldn't help himself.

One corner of her mouth shot up. Her dark locks whipped around her beautiful face, and it took all he was made of not to touch her, tuck her hair behind one ear.

Her cheeks were flushed from the chill, but tears were no longer streaming down. "I'm weel, but thank ye, Sir Xander."

"Just Xander." His voice cracked, so he cleared his throat. He wasn't a knight in the Realm of the Humans.

Lady Janet nodded.

Xander stared at her mouth, although he chided himself for it. He couldn't hear her thoughts. Calm washed over him as if she'd cast some sort of spell. Because of his gift, wondering what someone was thinking was uncommon, but definitely not an unwelcome change.

If this lass was like Alana and Angus, he should spend *more* time with her.

Peace.

Xander wanted peace.

He'd been lacking it since coming to the Isle of Skye.

"Are ye well?"

Her voice jolted him.

Xander straightened his shoulders. "You're crying, yet you're asking me if something's wrong? I should ask the same of you, my lady."

A bitter laugh greeted his ears, and Lady Janet shook her head. "I beg a' ye. Please dinnae." Her cheeks brightened with crimson, and she averted her gaze.

He frowned and again fought the urge to touch her. "As you wish."

Lady Janet's head shot up; her sapphire eyes wide. "Tha's it?"

Xander cocked his head to one side. "What?"

"Ye dinnae push me…like they do?" She gestured to the far-off castle.

"Nay." He shook his head. "I just want to see you smile."

Silence fell.

His honesty had shocked them both.

He squared his shoulders and shifted on his feet.

Why did I say that?

"I shall try." Lady Janet's voice was low, belying her words.

Xander reached for her hand; he couldn't help it.

She didn't pull away. Her eyes locked onto his face.

His pulse thundered in his ears. Something was burning his thigh through the pocket of his trews.

The ring.

Without releasing the lass, Xander dug in his pocket. A sense of rightness washed over him when his fingertips connected with the body-warmed Fae-forged metal.

He slid the bauble that his father's mother had given him as a child onto Lady Janet's ring finger.

She glanced at the ring, then back up at him.

"I'm sorry. I don't know why I did that." Xander's words were breathless to his own ears, and his heartbeat kicked up a notch. "You can take it off."

The black stone was oval and large, but the ring looked as if it belonged on her hand.

Xander had always assumed it was made of onyx. He couldn't tear his gaze away. His spine tingled, and his head spun.

Lady Janet lifted her hand from his and stared down at the piece of jewelry.

Then the stone flared orange. It melted into red, pulsating and glowing.

Magic made his body burn. Desire hit him in the gut and slid over him. An erection pushed against the fabric of his trews.

What in five hells?

A grunt fell from his lips; he ached for her. Needed to hold her, kiss her. Take her.

Lady Janet panted, her breasts heaving in her

navy-blue corset.

Sweat broke out on Xander's forehead despite the chill in the air.

The lass was suffering from the same condition, her face red and skin glowing from cheeks to neck, including the portion of her delicate collar bones he could see through the neckline of her leine. The glow inched up her arms and shoulders, slowly enveloping her, then crept to his boots, enclosing them both in a large aura-like bubble.

It was as if he'd cast a spell, but Xander wasn't in command of anything magical.

Alarm washed over him, but passion and drive won out when all he could see was the colors swirling around them both.

It had swallowed them whole.

Xander didn't fight the urge to pull her to him.

Lady Janet's palms landed on his chest. Seared through his doublet.

Their gazes collided.

He lowered his head and took her mouth.

She didn't fight him. Lady Janet pushed up to return his kiss, twining her tongue with his and slipping her arms around his neck.

Xander groaned and hauled her closer but tried not to crush her. Being Fae, he was much stronger. He couldn't—wouldn't—hurt her, even though his blood was singing in his ears. His temples throbbed as lust pounded its way through his form.

He was drowning in *her*.

His mind shouted that he needed to regain control, even as his body and his magic needed more.

What the hell is happening?

Xander felt something wrap around them both. His senses spiked. He ripped his mouth off hers, though she was still in his arms, plastered to his chest.

Magic surrounded them. Flowed *through* them.

A golden rope.

He could see it. Xander didn't have to squint. There it was, glowing. *Pulsing.* Different colors flashed over and spun around them, but the rope didn't waver.

Xander gasped, as did Lady Janet.

Can she see or sense it?

"What's happenin'? Why…what…a rope?" Her words were breathless, fragmented.

"You can see that?"

She nodded, her hair shifting with the movement. Her sapphire eyes were wide, and he tried not to look at her kiss-swollen lips.

Xander released her as chaos reigned in his mind. Dizziness spun his head, and his limbs shook. He locked his knees and sucked in air so he wouldn't fall over—or pass out. He pointed to the golden rope, not missing the fact that his hand was quaking. "That's a mating bond."

"What?"

"In human terms…you and I just got married."

chapter three

She fled.

It can't be.

His words *couldn't* be true.

Sir Xander had stood as if transfixed. He'd broken their physical contact, and Janet could no longer see what had to be magic. No more colors. No more rope.

Words had breached his lips. Unbelievable words.

Mated.

Bonded.

Married?

Janet's head reeled as the former Fae Warrior's declaration ran through her mind too fast to comprehend.

Sand bled to rocks under her feet. She was suddenly glad she'd borrowed a pair of boots from the stores. Her slippers would've had her falling on her face at the speed she was going.

Janet hiked her skirts higher, her heart pounding in her ears.

She'd left him there.

Standing on the beach, his cheeks flushed, lips swollen from her mouth.

How can this be?

Repeating the question didn't make it any clearer. No magic answer entered her thoughts.

Magic.

She'd *seen* it. Swirling colors, a large bubble surrounding them, cutting them off from the beach. Something that looked like a woven rope had wrapped around her hips, around the Fae man's, and then flowed *through* them both, even though she'd felt nothing.

Well, except for the hum in her whole body. Warmth encased her as sure as Xander's arms around her, his solid chest against her breasts. It'd been as if she was bare, his heat melting the feeling of the stiff bodice.

It hadn't been her first kiss, but a few stolen brushes of the miller's son's mouth against hers when she was a lass were nothing compared to how Xander had made her feel.

Janet had craved him. Craved more. She might be innocent, but she'd just learned what desire was.

The place between her legs still throbbed. Her thighs had trembled—her calves were still shaky. Janet fought the urge to collapse. She ran harder, until she darted through the gates, surprising her cousin Cormac, who stood guard.

He shouted after her, but Janet ignored him and kept going.

If Xander was in pursuit, she didn't see him when she glanced over her shoulder, but she could *sense* him. As if he was beside her. Janet could feel his heart beating steadily. Like their bodies were still melded.

Is that magic, too?

When she'd left him, the former Fae Warrior had had his hand to his forehead, those gorgeous violet eyes wide, as if he was just as confused as she. He'd muttered something in Fae—Janet guessed, because she'd not recognized all the words as her own Gaelic. However, one word was close to the Gaelic word for *fate*.

Sir Xander had reverted to his native language after Janet hadn't responded to his English.

Her heartbeat kicked up a notch.

Fate?

Janet didn't believe in fate.

Should she?

Her brother Duncan certainly believed it'd been Claire's destiny to come to him from the distant future. Alex believed the day he'd met Alana by chance had been fate.

Both twins *believed* the women they loved were *meant* to be theirs.

She paused in the great hall, sucking in air as her chest heaved. Janet fought the urge to cough as she caught her breath. She ignored the questions swirling around in her head about Sir Xander. "I dinnae believe in fate." Saying the words aloud didn't slow the chaos in her mind.

"What, lass?"

Janet startled. "Nothin', Mairi."

"Janet-lass?"

She met the dark eyes of the older woman in charge of the female servants. Mairi had been like a mother to Janet when she'd lost her own. She'd taught her how to run a household, but she'd been a friend as well as teacher.

Janet forced a smile.

"Did ye have a nice walk, lass?"

She nodded, squaring her shoulders, but that deep brown gaze still appraised. The shrewd one. The one that was good at catching mischievous laddies in a lie.

"Did somethin' happen?" Mairi wiped her hands on her apron, but her eyes never left Janet.

Aye.

"Nay." She smoothed her skirts. She'd lost her plaid somewhere along her run, but she'd worry about it later.

"Are ye sure, Janet?"

"Aye." She made her smile wider and brushed her hair back from her face.

Mairi's eyes honed in on the ring when Janet's hand was next to her cheek, but the older woman said nothing.

Janet's heart stuttered. She cleared her throat and scanned the great hall. Resisted the urge to hide her arms behind her back.

The fire was lit in the largest hearth, but there was no one else in the room. Three baskets of fresh rushes sat not far from the hearth. She'd interrupted Mairi's task.

Distraction is good.

"Do ye ken where my da is?"

Mairi nodded, a small smile curving her lips. "He's with tha laird in his ledger room."

"Thank ye."

"My ladies are both in the solar. Lady Alana was asking after ye, lass."

Janet forced another smile. "I shall seek them out." She nodded to Mairi and took her leave.

Alana and Claire were the last two people she wanted to see. However, the former princess was the logical choice. She knew more about magic than anyone Janet had ever met. Her sister-by-marriage could probably tell her all she needed to know about the ring on her finger.

Nay. I do not want to know.

Her body tingled. The ring caught her eye. It was changing color, going from red to purple. It swirled until settling into a deep blue.

"Aunt Janet!"

The young shout from across the great hall made her still before she could ascend the stairs. Her focus had been yanked from the piece of Fae jewelry on her hand—thankfully. Janet sucked in a breath and held it as she turned to her nephew.

Angus dashed to close the distance between them. He ignored the sharp, "How many times have I tol' ye? Dinnae run inside, lad," admonition from Mairi.

Janet didn't even get a chance to chide him for not listening to the housekeeper. His gaze focused on the Fae ring before she could meet his blue eyes.

The lad gasped and grabbed her hand. "Magic," Angus breathed.

Drat.

When their gazes collided, her nephew didn't look surprised. "I sense magic."

"Keep your voice down, lad."

"Where did ye get this, Aunt Janet?" Angus was unrepentant, as usual. Curiosity etched his expression, and he pulled her hand closer so he could stare at the stone, which now pulsed dark green.

"Release me. I must speak ta yer grandfa." She tugged, but Angus tightened his grip. If she told him she was headed to his mother, the lad would want to come.

Anything to do with magic fascinated her brother's son. He wouldn't take nay for an answer, and Janet had no desire to admit to someone so young she had accidentally—what, married?

"Nay, let me see it."

"Nay, let me go," Janet ordered. When her nephew looked back up at her, his mouth was set in a stubborn determined line. "Scoundrel," she muttered.

Angus flashed a grin that made him look so much like Alex, her irritation dissolved.

Considering her ire with both her brothers as of late, it was a surprise. Janet never could remain upset at the lad. He was her heart. "Since when is *scoundrel* a good thing to be called, lad?" She couldn't hold back a smile.

"Tell me where ye found this, Aunt Janet," Angus said, ignoring her tease.

"I dinnae find it." She rushed her words, sounding more like her nephew than herself.

"Where'd ye get it, then?"

"I gave it to her."

Janet's heart galloped. She'd not heard him enter the hall.

Xander stood not far, her lost plaid draped over his arm.

She had to swallow in order to breathe. Seeing the Fae man with MacLeod plaid on his body made her stomach flutter. "I've got ta go." Her words shook.

Angus cocked his head to one side, appraising her like Mairi had. The child was too perceptive for his own good.

"Here's your plaid, my lady." Xander crossed the distance and handed the fabric over.

Janet reached for it automatically. A bolt of energy shot up her arm when their hands brushed, and her cheeks heated. "Thank ye, Sir Xander. I'll take my leave. My da awaits."

"You and I must share words, my lady." His voice was firm, and his violet eyes locked onto her face.

She fought a shiver and stepped back. "I must go."

"'Tis urgent, lass." Xander dropped his voice.

Angus watched them, looking from one to the other as they spoke.

"As is my business with my father." Janet bowed from the waist, clutching her plaid with white knuckles even as she turned to flee up the wide staircase.

"What's wrong with my aunt, cousin?"

She winced when she heard Angus' question to the Fae man and kept going.

CHAPTER FOUR

lana's gasp made Janet close her eyes. The former princess turned her hand over and pulled it close like Angus had.

The lad hadn't appeared in the solar, so Janet wanted to thank Xander for keeping him busy — almost.

"I've not seen one of these in a very long time."

"What does tha' mean?" Janet asked, trying to suppress irritation at her sister-by-marriage's response.

"I sense that a family meeting is imminent." Claire flashed a grin before brushing her blonde locks from her face.

It almost hurt to look at Duncan's wife. She was radiant. Her gowns could no longer hide her pregnancy, as the bairn would come into the world in less than three months, and every day Claire looked even more beautiful. Janet had no doubt Alana would be the same way, although she was not yet showing.

"It's a special ring," the princess continued as if Claire had not spoken. Alana's refined tones spoke of her royal blood, but she sounded as Scottish as Janet did.

"A special ring?" Janet repeated.

"What does that mean?" Claire asked.

Janet frowned. She didn't want any witnesses to what she had to talk to Alana about, but she couldn't be rude to Claire. She pulled her hand from the princess' grip, refusing to look down at the ring. Her peripheral vision told her it was changing colors again—whatever that meant.

She tried not to pace in the bright warm room. The clouds had parted, revealing the sun as if even God was reveling in her—situation—with the Fae man.

"Your thoughts are chaotic," Alana said.

Janet didn't confirm or deny it when she met the Fae woman's eyes.

"Since when can you read minds?" Claire laughed.

"I cannot. The ring is showing me. Rapid swirls; different colors for different emotions. Calm, sister. Tell me what happened."

"Xander put tha ring on my finger." Her spine tingled when she said his name and Janet whipped away from both her sisters-by-marriage. She stared out of one of the many windows in the bright room.

"I'd gathered that, as the ring is Fae, and of great magic." Alana's voice was low and concerned. "Did he tell you what it means?"

"Aye." She nodded for effect since her back was to the former princess.

"What does it mean?" Claire asked.

Alana cleared her throat. "Shall I tell her, sister, or do you want to?"

Janet closed her eyes. "Ye can." Her voice cracked and her heart sped up.

"It means they are fated."

"What?" Claire gasped.

"As in we're s'pposed ta be mated—married." Janet clutched her hands behind her as she turned away from the window.

Claire's green eyes were wide. "Hot damn! Just when I thought I knew all about magic…there's always more. Congrats, Janet! Xander's a good dude."

Janet frowned. Though she'd heard the strange word before, it still took her mind a moment to process the speech.

Claire spoke oddly, but Janet had adored her from the moment they'd met, and she was teaching Claire Gaelic. Her sister-by-marriage had just joked that morning that perhaps she would eventually sound Scottish. She certainly hadn't just then.

Alana smirked, then stepped toward Janet. She reached for both her hands. "This does not have to be a bad thing, sister."

"So ye say."

Claire sat in the corner of the solar watching, rubbing her distended tummy.

The former princess nodded when Janet met her eyes again. The movement shifted her pale locks. Flaxen waves danced about her shoulders but flowed down to her hips.

Janet sucked in a breath. Xander's hair matched his

cousin's. She didn't want to think about him—or the ring on her finger. The stone caught her eye against her will. It was glowing blue again.

"My cousin is an honorable man. Kind. Gentle. Sweet."

Janet scoffed. "A sweet warrior?"

Even Claire nodded.

Her sisters-by-marriage were united against her.

But Xander is sweet.

Janet banished the memory of his mouth moving over hers. He'd held her to him lightly, tenderly, as if he'd been afraid to hurt her. However, as soft as his kiss had been, there had been great passion. She'd wanted to cling to him. Would have, too, had the former Fae Warrior not pulled away.

Was it the magic I saw?

Alana's violet eyes—also matching the man Janet was supposedly *destined* for—landed on her face. "Come now, sister. You know this to be true."

She did, but she wasn't about to admit it to her brother's wife.

The Fae woman grabbed her hand and squeezed. Those deeply hued eyes implored. "My cousin is dear to me. As dear as Alex and Angus, and the bairn growing inside me." Alana placed a palm over her slightly rounded belly.

Janet tried not to frown. She didn't need another reminder of what she didn't have. "I ken it," she whispered.

"He…he is broken, sister." Alana's eyes misted over.

Janet's heart skipped a beat she promptly ignored.

The former princess squeezed the fingers she still held. "You can fix him. All you have to do is love him. Please…heal Xander."

Shock washed over Janet, but she didn't get a chance to answer Alana.

Both of her brothers, her father, and her nephew burst into the solar.

Duncan had Xander by the arm. His grip looked tight, but if the Fae man was uncomfortable, his expression didn't let on.

"Duncan, be reasonable," their father, Iain, said.

"Ask fer her hand," Duncan demanded.

"Oh, geeze," Claire said. She grabbed the sides of the chair and awkwardly made it to her feet.

"Do it. Now!" Duncan yelled.

Alex threw his hands up in the air and stepped forward to pull his twin off Xander.

To Janet's supposed-husband's credit, his face remained placid while one brother ranted and raved and the other chided them both.

Good thing Alex was older than Duncan by several minutes and therefore the laird. Duncan had always been the hotheaded one, and Alex reasonable, and even-tempered.

Neither was pleasant to deal with if provoked, but in Janet's experience, that was just the plight of the

MacLeod male.

"Duncan." Her brother ignored her. "Duncan MacLeod!" Janet's shout still went unheeded as the men discussed her as if she wasn't in the room.

"The lass is trying to speak," their father said.

Both twins quieted but Duncan was tense, his broad shoulders as taut as his expression.

Xander stood between them, as muscled and broad as her six-and-a-half foot tall siblings.

Janet could feel his heart beat in time with hers.

When their eyes met, awareness darted all over her body and something tugged at her—almost physically. She swallowed.

Magic.

She couldn't see it, but there was no doubt she felt it. It would take a while to get used to.

"He dinnae have to offer for me," Janet said.

"The hell he dinnae," Duncan barked, unrepentant for such language in front of ladies. Her brother was furious. He turned to Xander again but didn't touch him—yet. "Ye took liberties wit' my sister. Ye shall marry her." He got in the former Fae Warrior's face.

Liberties? What did he tell them?

Janet's stomach fluttered.

"I've nay issue with such things." Xander's tone was calm.

"Guys, relax." Both males ignored Claire. She rested her hand on her husband's arm, and only then did Janet's brother take a step back.

As before, the former Fae Warrior appeared unruffled.

"Such *things*?" Janet snapped. "I'll dinnae have my future referred ta—" Her cheeks still burned from Duncan's declaration.

"The lass has a point," Alex said. His arms were crossed over his broad chest, and he leaned into the wall of the solar. "Marriage dinnae need ta be considered a formality."

Janet didn't relax, despite the laird's statement.

Angus watched, silently standing next to his father.

"This is about more than what they wish," Alana said. Her voice was firm but low, and all eyes of her overbearing family settled on the princess. "This is about fate."

"Destiny," Xander said.

"Nay!" Janet shouted. "'Tis abou' magic." She shook her head when two violet gazes zoned in on her.

Alana's smile was kind when she took a step toward Janet. "Nay, sister. The ring is but a method. It does not control the outcome." She shot a meaningful look to the males in the room. "As I would've explained, given the chance."

"The...outcome a' what?" Janet asked, her tummy quivering.

The former Fae princess shot a look at her son. "Angus, out. This conversation isn't for you, my love."

The lad made a face.

"Ye heard yer mother." Alex pushed off the wall. "Out wit' ye, laddie. Seek Mairi an' see if she needs help in the hall."

Angus's frown deepened, but he didn't argue with his father.

Alex rested his hands on his son's shoulders and guided him to the door.

Alana blew him a kiss and Angus dashed from the room.

If Janet knew her nephew, he wouldn't go far. He'd obey, but he'd offer to clean the walls in the corridor so he could overhear the conversation even though the solar door was shut.

Xander cleared his throat and Duncan glared his way.

Claire tugged her husband another step away from the Fae man.

Janet's heart sped up even before her supposed mate's—husband—gaze reached her.

He looked at Alana before those violet eyes settled on her again.

She tried not to fidget.

"As I understand it, the spell is to find my perfect mate. If you were not she, the magic would not have reacted."

"Aye," Alana whispered.

Janet's neck and cheeks seared.

Xander had spoken as if their kiss did not matter.

Had meant nothing.

It doesn't matter.

If that was so, why did his words—his expression—make her chest ache?

Iain whistled, but Janet couldn't look at her father. "Fae blood, I tell ye all, the Fae blood."

"Da." Alex groaned.

"He's right." Alana's affirmative made the throb of Janet's pulse in her temples thud harder.

"It's been *generations*." The statement came out cracked and Janet grabbed the back of the chair in front of her so she wouldn't fall over.

"Aye, but—" this time Duncan spoke. "I believe we have Fae blood."

Duncan believes?

Janet's head spun as her brother continued to speak.

"The seer needed my help ta open the Faery Stones. It worked because we are Fae, no matter how slight."

"Aye." Xander nodded.

He didn't sound surprised at Duncan's reference to his adventure six months before into the Fae Realm to retrieve Alana and their brother.

Aye? Just like that? Why is Xander so accepting of this?

Of…me?

Sweat broke out on her forehead. Janet's knuckles whitened until her fingers ached as she clutched the chair. The walls started to waver as if they were dancing. Then…as she watched, they slowly started to creep closer. Appearing as if they were actually moving, crushing the room. Her chest ached. She forced air into her body. Tremors chased each other down her spine and her legs trembled.

She needed to get away.

Flee.

Run, far away from the people in this room, smothering her.

Janet couldn't take Alana's imploring violet eyes.

She couldn't take both of her brothers hovering over her, or Duncan's threats to pound Xander if he didn't ask for her to be his wife.

Couldn't take Claire's wide, watching green eyes.

Janet *definitely* couldn't take her father's pleased expression.

How could the man be smug he'd been right about their Fae blood? The legend had been around for hundreds of years.

"I—"

Silence fell and they all looked at her.

Xander stared, his lips parted. As if he was about to say something but couldn't form the words.

Janet could feel the power pulsing between them again. She couldn't see it anymore, but she could suddenly feel the rope-like magic like she had when they'd been on the beach. She felt its weight at her hips, in her chest, as if Xander's hands were in both places.

Her heartbeat went from gallop to canter. She

fought the fuzziness in her head when her limbs warmed.

Without another word, she dashed from the room as Angus had before. She heard surprised exclamations from various family members.

Janet ignored them all.

She ran. Down the stairs. Across the great hall. Down the corridor and out of the entrance to Dunvegan. Didn't even breathe until she was past the bailey and beyond the gates.

Poor cousin Cormac called after her again, but Janet didn't stop for him either.

This will not be chosen for me.

chapter five

"Jesu. Now look what ye did." Duncan dragged his hand down his beardless face, then shoved his long dark hair over one shoulder.

Xander tried to ignore the tug of the magic between him and Janet.

He *needed* to go after her.

His heart pounded, and yet, there he stood by the laird and his brother, striving to act normally.

"Duncan, this isn't his fault." Claire frowned.

"Aye, but 'tis." The man, equal to Xander in breadth and height, looked down at his fair-haired wife. "If the Fae had kept his hands to himself, the lass wouldn't be in this predicament."

"Janet being revealed as mine *isn't* a predicament." Xander kept his words even, trying to ignore everyone's thoughts as the chaos of feelings and blame sped through his mind. Every emotion was a shout. Accusation, hostility, even the old laird's amusement and pleasure with the situation. Statements that made him dizzy. He winced.

"Yers?" Duncan spat the word as if a curse. "Dinnae the blame lay with ye? My sister fled. That speaks to how she feels for ye." He whirled around, stepping toward Xander again. The man got in his face; they were chest to chest, nearly touching.

"Brother, back up." Alex came closer, Alana on his heels.

Their father hovered near the door, looking amused instead of alarmed.

Alana reached for Xander, settling her hand on his forearm.

Blessed silence settled over his mind. It was *quiet*. He was alone in his own head, like when he'd been on the beach with the lass.

Considering the tension in the room, Xander couldn't chide his cousin for her unsolicited magical gift. "Thank you, cousin," he whispered.

She nodded, meeting his eyes, before looking up at her husband and brother-by-marriage. "I need to speak with my cousin. Alone."

Duncan frowned, but Claire nodded.

Alex squared his shoulders. "Verra weel, *mò chridhe*." He caressed Alana's cheek and pressed a kiss to her forehead.

Xander tried not to watch, or at least be detached, but he couldn't. He stared at the tenderness the laird displayed for Alana and couldn't erase Janet's blue eyes from his mind.

He'd touched her. Knew how her skin felt beneath his fingertips. Remembered her taste and how it was to have her up against his chest, in his arms. Xander had to swallow hard.

Duncan leaned in, sticking one thick finger in his face. Sapphire eyes — matching his sister's — narrowed. "Ye *will* make this right."

"Duncan." Claire's sharp admonition was ignored, but the man did back away.

He threw his arm around his pregnant wife's shoulders. "Ye need ta rest, *mò gradh.*" His tone was gentle, as if he'd not been ferocious moments before.

"Yeah, I *was.*" Claire rolled her eyes.

Alex chuckled as he followed them out of the room. "Come, Da." He gestured to his father. "We've a meetin' with the steward. We've already kep' him waiting."

Iain nodded.

When the door closed, Xander tried to avoid his cousin's gaze, but couldn't. She might be diminutive in stature, but he'd never been able to look away when she commanded his attention.

One of the few situations Alana used her former rank to her advantage.

No matter where they were now, he couldn't discard how he'd been raised to treat her. Respect was ingrained. It just so happened affection for his cousin was, as well.

"I'd ask what you were thinking, but I don't think you were. As unusual as that is…" Alana kept her voice low, but Xander heard slight amusement, too.

He sighed and shook his head. "Nay. Magic drove me. I didn't recognize what was happening until it was too late."

Alana laughed.

"What is amusing, cousin?"

She took a seat and motioned for him to sit beside her. Both chairs rested in front of the fireplace.

Peat tickled his nose. Fresh and earthy, making the room smell as if they were outside. He glanced at the welcoming fire, burning low and hot as it consumed the block of moss.

So different from home.

It wasn't unpleasant, but Fae burned scented woods grown from special trees. They were sweet, filling the air with the aromas akin to sugary confections baking. The fires were also colored, depending on what wood was being used.

"Nothing is truly amusing, Xander. Your tone speaks of dread."

"I cannot deny that."

Alana took his hand and squeezed. "She is for you."

He couldn't find his voice, so he just closed his eyes, giving in to a reluctant nod.

A human mate?

She laughed again. His cousin wore a charming smirk when their gazes met again. "*My* human mate is more than enough."

He'd spoken aloud?

Bollocks.

Xander had no rebuttal as he tried *not* to look into

Alana's violet eyes.

"Xander, please." Her voice dropped. "Do not fight this, cousin. 'Twill only make you ill."

She was right, but he wasn't going to admit it aloud. The legend of rings like his — Janet's now — was that it *found* your perfect mate — a soulmate, humans would say. He'd had it so long, Xander didn't remember much, but he did recall his grandmother's words as she'd pressed it into his young palm.

The couple must do the rest.

The problem was the magic *expected* both parties to comply. Illness — or worse — could result if either fought the mating bond.

The bond itself had little to do with the ring's spell. Only those truly meant to be together could form the golden rope linking them. Rare among the Fae. To bond with a human? Xander hadn't known it was *possible* until that morning.

A new mating bond needed to be solidified by physical consummation. It would never go away, even if it wasn't, but their lives — if they both survived — would be unpleasant, to say in the least. Full of pain and yearning.

He'd always carried the ring with him, but he'd never believed in its magic. At least, Xander had never expected there was a match for his soul.

Especially away from the Realm of the Fae.

"I don't want to fight it." The words surprised him, but they were true. "I would just prefer she wanted the pairing as well." *Also, true.* Xander swallowed.

"Give her time, love." Alana's shoulders relaxed and she offered a small smile. "This is a shock to you *both*. To the whole family, actually."

His cousin considered him *family*, of course. Now…he was also family to Clan MacLeod.

Family.

Love.

The endearment from Alana wasn't wholly unusual, but why did Janet's smile pop into his mind?

Alana laughed and Xander arched an eyebrow.

"Oh, Xander, I'm so happy you want to be loved." The princess' magic included empathic powers. One more power that wasn't diminished for her in the Human Realm. "Janet is beautiful, inside, and out. Perfect for you."

His heart stuttered, and he tried to frown. "Suddenly I know what it is to have my mind invaded."

His cousin flashed an unrepentant grin. "I cannot help it when you think so loudly, but it's a relief."

"To have my greatest fears and desires voiced? I think not."

The former princess giggled like a lassie and threw her arms around him.

Xander felt a chuckle break from his lips, and he gathered his cousin close. She'd always been free with her love for him, much to the chagrin of their Fae Elders.

"I've been so worried about you since we've come here." Alana's words muffled against his chest.

"I know." Xander locked his jaw to keep unwanted emotion at bay.

"Thank you for coming here. You gave up everything for me."

He pulled back and tilted her face up. Xander thumbed a tear away as it trickled down her cheek. "Nay. Don't weep for me. Never that."

Alana's mouth curved in a watery smile. "'Tis the bairn. She makes my emotions wild." Her expression slid into radiant as she straightened, resting a hand on her stomach.

"She? You know already?"

His cousin nodded. "Aye. I've told Alex just this morning. We're going to call her Alexandria."

Xander smiled. "A great honor to be named after her father. He is a good man. A good husband and father, as well as leader to his people."

She gripped his hands and squeezed. "I love him, Xander. More than life. And my bairns. He's given me a strong beautiful lad, and my daughter will be the same, I've no doubt. I feel her magic inside me already. Angus and my daughter-to-be are the best of *both* worlds. I want this for you. You've always been more like a brother to me than protector or cousin. Please…"

A lump formed in his throat at the plea in her violet eyes. Alana was hurting *for* him, and it stole his breath. He wanted to promise her that it would all be fine. That he and his reluctant mate would find the love she and the laird shared.

Xander couldn't.

He wouldn't force the lass to be with him, despite what was supposed to be their destiny. "I will not fight this. That is the only vow I can make to you right now."

Alana beamed.

"This pleases you, cousin?"

She nodded. "The rest will be as it should."

He studied her. Xander didn't need to be an empath to sense her confidence, satisfaction. "I couldn't give you the words you wanted."

"But you did. Above all, you've always been an honest man. *And* I have faith in you."

Xander shook his head but didn't fight his smile. If only Janet would agree, and not fight their infant bond. His stomach fluttered at the thought of her getting sick or dying because of him.

He reached mentally for the magic between them. Xander sensed her down on the beach, but he couldn't feel what she was feeling. He'd been told most bonded mates — as rare as they were in the Fae Realm — could not only read each other's minds but had empathic abilities where their mate was concerned.

Thinking and feeling as one.

Could he hope for that deep of a connection with a human lass?

Xander rose and strode to one of the many windows in the warm bright room. His cousin let him go. No doubt Alana could sense that he needed some space between them.

The MacLeod soldiers and men-at-arms were once again sparring in the bailey.

Goddess knows Duncan MacLeod needs it.

Especially if Xander was to remain unscathed.

He would've let the man hit him if it'd come to that. Xander would never lift his hand to his cousin's family.

My family now.

Duncan and Alex were his brothers-by-marriage already by Fae standards. If Janet wished a wedding as Alana had, they'd be family by human customs as well.

Right.

If I can convince the lass not to reject me.

When his cousin gasped, he glanced over his shoulder. "What—?"

Alana had gone pale.

Xander started to cross the room to her but stopped in his tracks. Magic skittered down his spine and made his head spin.

Something yanked at his mating bond with Janet.

Then she was gone.

I can't feel her.

At. All.

Panic crept up from his gut, and he wobbled on his feet.

Alana met him in the middle of the solar. Her hand shot out to steady him, and their eyes locked.

"Janet," Xander breathed.

"The Faery Stones," Alana said at the same time.

chapter six

Janet ran hard.

Harder than she had when she'd fled Xander on the beach. Her legs and lungs burned equally, and her throat was dry. Her ears stung from the rushing wind, and she shivered against the chilled air, despite the heat she'd worked up from exertion.

She paused, leaning on a boulder to catch her breath. Closed her eyes. "What am I goin' ta do?" Her words were desperate to her ears, and she clenched her jaw until her teeth ached. It did nothing to stave off tears.

As they coursed down her cheeks, a warm contradiction to the cool wind, she started to rock, bumping into the large slab over and over. The rough surface bit into her shoulders and upper back, but the pain was good. It grounded her.

She looked around. Janet was so far from Dunvegan she couldn't see the castle over the crest of the hills.

"Drat." She'd never been this far down the beach.

Certainly not alone.

Cormac had wanted to accompany her when she'd gone out this morning. He'd only considered letting her out of the gates by herself because Xander was already on the beach in the first place. Janet hadn't run into the former Fae Warrior when she'd ventured down to the water. Not until he'd joined her.

Normally when she left the safety of Dunvegan, if either of her brothers couldn't accompany her, one of their men, usually a cousin, did so. It was irritating to be watched by men all the time, even if they proclaimed to care about her.

If she kept going, she'd run into MacDonald land. The rival clan's stronghold, Armadale, was on the other side of Skye but their lands and those who were beholden to them met. MacDonald beaches picked up where MacLeod beaches left off. Their clans had warred for years. The peace they had currently was put in place by her father and the current Laird MacDonald's father and could be considered tentative at times.

Janet shivered for reasons other than the weather. "That, I dinnae need."

Clans MacLeod and MacDonald had been rivals forever—but true enemies for about a hundred years due to a botched marriage.

She could've laughed at the irony, but she needed to go back.

Neither of her brothers could stand the current Laird MacDonald. It would be just like the unmannered couth, Hugh, to grab her for ransom if he saw her on the beach, too. Rumor had it he could often be seen riding the border of his lands on a giant black stallion.

Janet sucked in one breath, then another.

There was a crack in the ridge behind her, forming a crevice in the face of the wall-like cliff that probably led to a cave. She was tempted to fit her body into the darkness there and hide — forever.

Janet had been craving a man, a husband for years.

Now she had one.

A stranger, despite the fact she'd known him for six months.

"How can I face him?"

Don't have a choice, really.

Not if what Alana and Xander had said about the bond was true.

It's no different than if Da or Alex arranged a match.

Right?

Nay.

Janet shook her head. She didn't want a man who didn't want her. She wanted a man who could love her. Give her children. Hold her —

But…Xander held me.

He'd kissed her. Caressed her. Left her wanting *more.*

She could go to him. Give herself to him. He was capable of giving her a bairn, she had to assume. If he never loved her, Janet would be content with loving his child, wouldn't she?

Nay.

Her bottom lip trembled. She wanted a man to

look at her like Duncan looked at Claire. Like Alex looked at Alana. Not a man who was forced into some magical bond.

Perfect mate?

Janet squared her shoulders and straightened her back. She couldn't run away, not really.

What good is hiding from a problem?

"I'm a MacLeod. I'm stronger than this. I'm goin' home."

She pushed off the boulder and clenched her jaw.

Mairi always said everything happened for a reason. Could her bond with Xander be the same?

What's the reason?

Suddenly, her limbs were not her own.

Something pulled at her. Janet tried to walk forward, but more than sand and rock offered resistance. Wind buffeted her skirt. It was born from nowhere, a strong gale that had her clutching at the boulder so she wouldn't fall over. Her hair whipped in her eyes, and she couldn't spare a hand to move it so she could see. Her arms strained until white-hot pain shot all the way into her shoulders, but she lost the battle to hold on.

Janet screamed as her body rose into the air. Her limbs pin-wheeled. She went *up* instead of down.

The ring burned her finger, as if it was new and hot from the smith's smelting tools. The stone pulsed red. This time, it was as if it was angry, not the same as the hue it'd been when the bond with Xander had been initiated.

She screamed again, but the sound was torn from her mouth.

Janet fell.

Everything went black.

"I'm goin' with ye." Duncan's booming voice jolted Xander as he shoved supplies into a hide bag.

Alana was supposed to have been the only one to enter his private quarters with him.

Xander heard a claymore clear its sheath.

A MacLeod invasion.

"Nay," Alana said. "Tis too dangerous." His cousin had followed him down to the kitchens to procure a sennight's worth of food, as well as been by his side as he'd readied personal items and gathered weapons.

Xander was happy to let her deal with her — *their* — brother-by-marriage.

"'Tis too dangerous for ye, as well, *mò chridhe*," the laird said. He stood near his brother.

Alex and Duncan had never stepped foot inside Xander's rooms. Until today.

"I'm no' going to cross over," Alana said.

Xander gave into a slight smile. His cousin was starting to sound more MacLeod and less Fae.

"I've need to make sure there's nothing wrong

with the Faery Stones. Janet shouldn't have been able to open them."

"Maybe she didn't." Xander tied the bag shut and straightened.

Both twins frowned as he turned and swept his eyes over them.

He looked at Alana. "I can open the Stones myself. I don't need you to come."

Stubbornness flashed across her countenance. "'Tis perfectly safe for me to go down to the beach. I am carrying a bairn; I'm not fragile. Besides, I've been with child before. There are no worries for me or my daughter."

Alex grunted and narrowed his eyes but didn't argue with his wife.

Xander arched an eyebrow. "As you wish."

His cousin nodded curtly and crossed her arms over her chest.

He bit back a smirk. They'd not win against that look on her face, even united. Alana, true to her royal blood, did not like to be ordered about.

"We've all been to the Realm of the Fae," Duncan said. "We ken what ta expect. I'm goin' with ye."

"Nay." Xander squared his shoulders. "Fae sense humans. You know this. I must go alone. I can only hope my bond with Janet masked her in some form."

Alana's tight expression shouted her doubt, but she didn't give voice to any fears.

"So, ye think I'm goin' ta leave the fate a' my sister

in yer hands? The Fae think ye a traitor!" Although Duncan's words were logical, they still had some bite.

Xander winced. "I know. I'll get her and return as quickly as I can. I must avoid capture as well."

"Her fate is in his hands anaway," Alex said.

Duncan glared even harder as his twin continued. "They're destined, remember?"

Alana smiled and reached for her husband's hand.

"Ye *will* wed her tha moment ye return," Duncan barked.

Xander nodded. "If she wishes it."

"Dinnae *only* if she wishes it." Duncan's dark brows drew tight.

"Come now, brother," Alex protested. "I shall no' force her. As laird, 'tis my place to make the decision. Our *sister* chooses."

Duncan scowled but didn't argue with his twin.

Xander's already deep respect for Alex MacLeod increased. "Thank you." His voice cracked and he cursed it.

The laird gave a brusque nod, a smile playing at his lips as he entwined his fingers with Alana's.

His cousin stood tiptoed and kissed her man's cheek. She whispered something in his ear that made his smile slide into a grin.

Xander had to look away. "We waste time. I must go."

Duncan argued all the way down the beach as they trudged to the small cave disguised in the cliff-side.

Worry for his new wife dominated Xander's mind, but it helped block out Duncan's words, as well as the man's dark thoughts.

The entrance to the place where the Faery Stones were hidden would fool any passersby that there was anything other than a split in the cliff face. It was slender enough that Alana would be the only one of their group who wouldn't have to turn sideways to enter. The opening led to a sizable cavern, containing the only known gate into—and out of—the Fae Realm.

Alana kept the area warded with a strong spell, so it was a wonder Janet could've come close, even by accident. The spell was supposed to make anyone in the area be overcome with apprehension and dread. A magical '*Stay Out!*' sign.

It was also supposed to feed confusion and memory loss once the person moved away, so they wouldn't remember the area and tell anyone of their mysterious instance on the beach of Skye.

Only one of Fae Blood could open it. His cousin believed it operated differently if one was not of pure blood. A halfling, an Irish lass named Bridei, had caused the rift in time that brought Claire to 1672 Scotland.

Xander's heart thundered.

Janet didn't have enough Fae blood to be considered a halfling, but what if she wasn't in the Fae Realm?

What if she's been sucked through time?

Alana shot him a sharp look as they wound their way through the small opening in the ridge. "What is it, cousin?"

Xander whispered his fear to the former princess when the four of them spilled into the cavern.

The twins exchanged a look neither he nor Alana acknowledged.

She shook her head. "Nay, Xander. I think the ring opened the Stones. Perhaps it tried to return home since its task was complete. Do you know if your father's mother or her mother put a return spell on it?"

"I don't know." He swallowed.

"You'll find her. I just hope when she arrived, Janet ran into the forest."

"I do as well." Xander's words were choked.

"The lass is smart. An' she's heard us speak of tha realm," Duncan said, but his voice was thick, worried.

Alex felt the same way. His expression—and his thoughts—mirrored his brother's.

The king kept guards at the Fae Realm's Stones in the Field of Light at all times.

What if they'd killed her?

Nay.

Xander ignored the way his heart plummeted to his stomach. Was that the reason he could no longer feel their bond?

His cousin squeezed his arm and shook her head. As if she'd read his mind.

He couldn't muster a tease since *he* was the mind

reader. His blood had run cold. Even if Janet wasn't meant to be his, a lone *beautiful* human lass wouldn't fare well amongst Fae Warriors.

Not all of his former brethren were honorable. They were bred to fight. Even the lower castes of the winged soldiers were ruthless.

Rape.

The word bounced around in Xander's head. He growled to himself and gripped the hilt of his Fae-forged sword. He'd show them what *traitor* truly meant if any one of them laid a hand on his fated mate.

"Let's get on wit' it, then," Duncan said.

Alana nodded to her brother-by-marriage and slid closer to the Faery Stones, her husband on her heels. "I hope the alarm did not sound when she arrived."

"They probably sensed her arrival, anaway, dinnae?" Alex asked.

"Aye, I fear so," Xander murmured.

Five clustered natural formations rose from the cavern's floor, perfectly spaced from each other, in a loose circle. One was centered, and the other four encircled it. A Fae, magic-born crystal sat atop each rough pillar, the one in the center larger than the rest. It was the key to making the others work. They had to be in tune as a whole to open the portal.

Even before Alana put her hands on the center crystal, it lit up, as if welcoming her to its side. A hum filled the cavern, the other crystals also lighting in order and starting to hum. The wind born of the Faery Stones as well as his cousin's magic whipped her gown around her body and her pale locks around her face. The laird stood behind her, his hands on her waist to steady her, although Alana probably didn't need Alex's touch.

Xander watched as the crystals grew more radiant by the second, brightening the cave around them, making them all squint.

"Ye'll bring her back?" Duncan grunted from where he stood next to him.

"Aye."

A loud *pop* sounded. Colors began to swirl in the air as an orb shot out from the stones, rotating, and growing wider and wider. The portal was hazy as it slowly opened.

Xander couldn't see through it yet, but in moments it would be a window, the other side visible. His heart kicked up. He'd have his wings again. His magic would be at full capacity. He'd assumed he would never again visit the land of his childhood.

Thought he would never fly again.

"Safely?" Duncan had to shout as the air whistled through the contained area of the cavern.

"Aye!" Xander nodded, flexing his grip on the hilt of his sword.

"Keep yer hands ta yerself, while yer at it."

He smirked at the scowl on his new brother-by-marriage's face. "She's my mate."

"Dinnae be so yet," the man barked.

"She is by Fae standards."

"Dinnae by *MacLeod* standards."

Xander bowed at the waist. "You have nothing to worry about."

Duncan harrumphed, crossing his arms over his broad chest.

The haziness of the portal cleared, and Xander could see the bright orange and blue grass. Purple and pink-topped Acana trees waved in a breeze across the field behind the dais the other realm's Faery Stones were perched upon. They were a matching set to the Stones here.

The air of serenity before him was false, even though no one was visible. His uncle was not a fool. The Faery Stones never went unguarded. Soldiers—either winged or not—were no doubt poised to attack.

Xander's heart rate sped up.

Janet.

Where was the lass?

His lass.

Xander needed to go. Now.

Alana threw her arms around him in a quick hug.

He pressed a kiss to her forehead.

"Be safe and quick, cousin," she whispered.

Xander nodded.

Alex grabbed his forearm and squeezed. "Godspeed, brother."

He was taken unawares by the sincerity in the laird's blue eyes. Xander had to swallow again and forced another nod. He locked his knees when they wobbled. His chest was tight.

Brother.

Even amongst Fae Warriors, the word was not used lightly.

His cousin's husband had accepted him. As match for his sister and considered him a brother. *Welcomed* family member.

Xander had no idea how much he'd craved the inclusion until the laird had said the word.

Alana's eyes went misty as she picked up the sentiment and probably her husband's feelings.

Alex's thoughts told Xander he'd read his expression, but for once he didn't mind picking up someone's unsaid words. The laird smiled and offered a nod.

Duncan also clutched his arm.

Their gazes collided.

"Bring my sister back. I trust ye to do tha'. Then I'll call ye brother."

"We'll be back. Together."

chapter seven

She landed on her hands and knees.
Hard.

Pain shot up her wrists into her arms, and into her thighs. Janet winced.

The grass beneath her fingertips was…orange? Bright and unnatural.

Did I hit my head?

Pushing to her feet, agony in her right ankle buckled her knee, and she cried out. Janet extended her arms for balance and managed not to fall backwards but clutched at what looked like a dais in front of her.

Realization hit and she blinked again.

She looked up at what had to be the Faery Stones. Janet had never seen them before, but they appeared pretty much how her sister-by-marriage had described them. Five pillar-like rocks forming a circle, each with a large crystal on top. Stalagmites, Claire had called them.

These were not the Faery Stones she'd been told were in a cave on the beach. There was no beach in sight.

No Isle of Skye. No waters.

Not to mention the orange and blue grass.

I'm in the Fae Realm.

Oh. God.

The curse was born, something Janet had admonished Angus for many times—but it was more plea, prayer, than taking the Lord's name in vain.

How did I get here?

She looked around, running through every word Alana and Claire had told her about the Realm of the Fae.

Colors, all deeply hued and unnatural, like the ground cover, surrounded her. The tree canopy of the nearby forest was pink and purple. The trunks of the same trees were various shades of red. The tall grass of the field was blue, the shorter blades orange.

Her heart bounced against her ribcage as her instincts screamed.

Run.

Hide.

Janet whimpered. Her brothers—and Sir Xander— had often talked about the fierceness of the winged Fae Warrior class.

"I need to go."

But where?

She scanned the field before her. The trees moved in a pleasant breeze that shifted her skirts and her hair, as if the forest was beckoning.

It was warm—much more so than the beach on Skye. The sun was bright, not hiding behind fluffy clouds like it had been at home. In the distance a vast palace was visible.

Janet shuddered. Wherever she went, she wouldn't head there.

Home. She wanted to go home.

There was no one in sight.

Where are all the soldiers?

Hadn't Alana mentioned how she couldn't return to the Fae Realm if she'd wanted to, since her father had the Stones on his side guarded day and night alike?

Panic inched up from Janet's gut. Her arms and legs shook. She took a step, then faltered. Her ankle screamed a protest as she steadied herself, barely managing to stay on her feet. Tears—of fright and pain—stung her eyes. Her gaze shot to the right when a twig snapped.

He saw her at the same time she saw him.

A Fae Warrior.

Long dark hair in a thick plait. A sword the same size as her brothers' claymores sheathed at his waist. He wore a dark green, shiny chest-plate.

Janet screamed.

He drew his sword and started shouting words she didn't understand. It sounded like Gaelic, but the words were off. She didn't take the time to concentrate to see if she could comprehend anything. No matter what he was saying, it wasn't friendly.

His iridescent wings flexed. Sunlight glinted off them like a prism.

Two more winged Fae men landed in the orange

and blue grass.

Janet's eyes darted between the forest and the soldiers. She would have to pass them to disappear into the trees. She'd never make it on her injured foot. Frustrated and helpless tears spilled down her cheeks as she backed up. White-hot pain shot into her knee, but she kept going until the wood of the dais hit her shoulder and hip at the same time.

Wind was born from nowhere and the Fae Warriors turned collectively, looking up.

Janet's skirts were plastered to her legs and the sleeves of her leine flapped against her upper arms, making her shiver. Gooseflesh rose and she had to squint when her hair whipped around her face.

She couldn't see the Faery Stones, but she could *hear* them. A lyrical, rhythmic hum reverberated, becoming louder every second.

The Warriors' shouts were frantic. The other two drew swords. They formed a line, gesturing to each other, taking no notice of her.

What's happening?

Although it just about killed her, Janet didn't stand idle. She took advantage of the soldiers' distraction. She darted around the dais and slid behind it, uttering curses she'd heard her brothers moan when a wound from the fighting yard required a poultice or to be sewn up. Men were like bairns when they bled.

Janet could still see the three Fae Warriors, but they likely couldn't see her.

Colors swirled in the air. There was a loud shredding noise, then another, like parchment ripping. She winced and ducked down, though squatting hurt her ankle even more. She clutched the plank of wood before her, praying the portal would stay open—if that was what was happening.

Maybe I can go home.

Some sort of bubble-magic, like the one that had surrounded her and Xander on the beach, popped into existence and slowly opened up; she could see through this one. It was dark on the other side, but she could make out what looked like rocks.

The cave?

Someone walked through the bubble, blocking her view, then lowered himself to the ground, hand on the hilt of a sword. He was still hazy, but awareness skittered down her spine.

Xander.

Janet's gasp was ripped from her mouth in the moving air. The bubble—or the portal—disappeared with another loud *pop.*

He crouched, but his eyes locked onto her at the corner of the dais, as if he'd heard her thinking his name. "Janet!"

Xander's voice made her shake. Janet couldn't move, even as her so-called-husband yelled for her. She should go to him.

"Stay there. I'm coming for you."

She nodded, clutching the wood until her knuckles

whitened.

Xander straightened, raising his arms, and yelling something. With a burst of multi-colored light, wings appeared on his back. His expression was triumphant.

The three Fae Warriors shouted.

One took to the air, but instead of attacking, he flew away.

Janet's gut told her he was going to get reinforcements.

Xander drew his sword and whipped his other hand around, throwing a fiery blue ball of light at the other two Warriors.

They scattered, one taking to the air to move away. The magic disappeared, missing both of them.

"Traitor!" The shout was English and made Janet shake even more.

When Xander flew, she watched in mesmerized fright as his newly appeared wings pumped hard, moving him higher.

He's drawing them away from me.

Should she run?

No, he'd told her to stay put. So, Janet would obey.

She couldn't look away.

The first clash of swords made her whimper and bite her bottom lip. Sword fighting she'd seen.

But…in the air?

The bright sun made it difficult to see everything. Janet squinted, staring at the three moving figures.

Xander parried and dove, throwing fiery balls as

he fought, but so were the other two winged soldiers. They came together and moved away in some morbid dance full of magic and swords. They were yelling, too, in that close-to-Gaelic language.

Her breath caught, her mouth going dry as the two Warriors descended on Xander together. One shot forward to wrap around her supposed-husband's torso, the other going for his legs. They pinned his arms down, his sword hanging helplessly in his hand. He struggled in their hold, and suddenly the three figures were plummeting toward the ground.

Janet's heart beat so hard she feared it would stop.

Xander tried to yank away, but the other two Fae held tight as they slowed, pumping their wings in tandem. She could feel the magic between her and Xander, like she had on Skye, but Janet couldn't see it.

The three Fae men rolled to the ground as one. As if on purpose.

A calculated capturing move.

"Nay," Janet whispered.

What if they killed him?

A burst of light so bright she had to look away erupted from Xander and his captors.

She cried out. Janet shook from head to foot. Had she just seen the man she was supposed to be destined for murdered with magic?

Tears burned her eyes and her bottom lip trembled, so she bit down on it. When the radiance faded and her vision cleared, Xander was striding toward her. She frantically searched for the other two Warriors, but they lay on the orange and blue grass, unmoving.

Xander sheathed his sword and smiled when their eyes met.

Her gaze drank him in the closer he got. Janet needed to say something—anything—but her voice was gone. Her throat dry, she didn't try.

He jogged to close the distance between them.

She could see no marks on his body, and no blood. His leine was ripped on one sleeve, but he didn't appear to be injured.

Thank God.

A breath Janet hadn't realized she'd been holding rushed from her lips.

When he reached for her, she put her hand in Xander's without hesitation.

Magic hit her in the chest, but it wasn't unpleasant. Her whole body warmed, starting in her heart, and sliding down her arms, her legs, even her fingers and toes. Her stomach fluttered. Janet stumbled, head spinning.

Xander steadied her, drawing her into his arms. "That's our bond. You'll feel it more here, especially when we touch. Magic is alive in this realm."

"I—"

"We need to go. We can talk when we get to safety. I've only stunned them. Reinforcements will be here shortly. We cannot get captured."

She didn't have the guts to ask where safety could be. "I want to go home."

"I do not have enough time to open the Stones. Are you hurt?"

"A-a-aye."

His violet eyes bored into her, and a tremor shot down her spine. "Did they touch you?" It was a growl that made her shiver even more.

"Nay." Janet shook her head. "'Tis my ankle. I dinnae ken how."

Xander pulled her closer and she couldn't help it, she burrowed into his chest, slipping her arms around his waist. She hugged him to her, and he squeezed her right back.

Janet closed her eyes against his shoulder, trembling as emotions swirled in her head. She felt *right* in his arms, but still scared out of her wits.

His heart beat in time with hers. She could feel it against her breasts, but it was *more* than that. Like before, it was as if his pulse was in her body with her own.

"I've got you, lass." Xander's warm breath kissed her temple, and she couldn't help but remember his mouth moving over hers at the beach.

"I'm frightened," Janet whispered.

"Aye, I am, too. We need to go."

Janet lifted her head, and their gazes collided. "I dinnae be able ta walk, Xander." It was the first time she'd said his name without an honorific, but somehow it, too, felt right.

"You won't have to." He flexed his wings.

"Flying?" Anticipation and dread slipped down her spine. Flying was…unnatural. She'd never been fond of heights.

"Aye. Hold onto me; I'll never drop you." Xander dipped his head down and pressed his mouth to hers in a hard kiss.

Janet swallowed a gasp. The brush of his lips on hers was over before she'd had time to react, but her body heated, and her heart thundered even faster. She would've kissed him back, like she had on the beach of Skye.

Why?

Was magic making her lose her head to this man?

Or is it more?

She ignored that, shoving it to the back of her mind.

Nonsense.

She might have known who he was for the past six months, but Janet didn't know Xander.

Not really.

Without another word, he pumped his wings twice, then a third time.

Her trembling started when he slowly rose into the air. Janet gasped and tightened her grip on his waist. As soon as they were completely off the ground, she wound her legs around his calves, wincing when her ankle shot pain into her knee.

Janet felt the rumble in his broad chest that had to be a laugh, but Xander held her closer.

"I promise I won't drop you, lass."

"I dinnae look down." She hid her face in his neck.

He chuckled again.

Janet felt his lips on her forehead and smiled despite herself. Chilled air slid over her form, at odds with the heat of his body against hers, his warm strong embrace around her.

"Do what you must; I'll do the rest."

"Thank ye," she whispered as the wind rushed in her ears, whipping her hair as they moved higher.

"You're mine to protect."

Janet didn't answer, and she ignored how much she liked the words. She squeezed her eyes shut and held onto Xander as he soared even farther into the air.

chapter eight

There was only one place Xander could take her. One place the Fae avoided like the plague. Grànnda Falls.

Grànnda meant *ugly* in Fae and Gaelic alike, and the Falls, and the woods around them were the only geographical area of the Fae Realm where the foliage was the muted greens and browns of the Human Realm. No purple and pink Acana trees. No blue-barked Subh trees or a blade of orange grass in sight, let alone of the soft wavy blue variety.

No one seemed to know why the colors were so different from the rest of the realm. It was rumored that the area was cursed. There didn't seem to be an origin story even in the vast library of the palace. It was also feared that the place sucked magic away, but that was nonsense.

The Falls' foliage was what Janet would consider normal.

Xander's people, on the other hand, considered the vast Falls, surrounding forest, and the river undesirable. A shame, really, since the Grànnda Falls area had some of the best hunting in the realm.

Even if they burned through the supplies he'd

brought, they wouldn't starve.

They would have to be careful because there were Fae living in the area—several exile camps in the vast forest around the Falls. He and his mate would have to avoid being seen by outcast Fae as well as anyone else.

He shuddered and hoped it didn't translate to the lass in his arms. Xander didn't think they'd survive more than a few days undiscovered, let alone a whole week.

King Fillan would have patrols out to find them. They would search high and low. Wouldn't give up until Xander and Janet were captured. They needed to formulate a plan and get back to the Faery Stones. Back to the Human Realm.

Xander had said an invisibility spell the moment they'd left the two unconscious Fae Warriors and he hoped to the Goddess it held. He probably should've killed Mikhias and Ruark but getting away had been more important. A part of him hadn't wanted Janet to see him kill, either.

He stretched his wings and rose even higher, hitting a thermal and gliding. The warm air caressed his newly returned iridescent appendages and his face, ruffling his clothing, mussing his hair, and making him grin.

His magic was back.

Full force and screaming in his mind, running in his blood.

Xander threw his head back, closed his eyes and

laughed. Had Janet not been wrapped around his body, he would've thrown his arms out and floated backwards. Perhaps even performed backflips in the air like he had as a lad. He wanted to shout for joy.

When he felt her tremble in his grip, he met her gaze. He might not be able to read her mind, but her sapphire eyes were wide, her arms and legs tight around him.

As much as Xander was reveling in being in the air, his mate was panicked. His elation deflated and he rubbed her back. "Not much further, and we'll be there."

"Where?" Her voice shook.

Xander held her tighter if it was possible. He wanted to kiss her, touch her, but even if they were in a safe situation, something told him his would-be-wife would never be comfortable in the air. Plus, she was injured.

Which makes me a wretch.

"Grànnda Falls."

"Ugly?" Janet arched one dark brow.

He grinned. "Aye. You'll see why."

She stayed plastered to him, hiding her face as their journey continued.

Xander heard the Falls before he could see them. The forest was overgrown and lush; the tree canopy would be adequate shelter if they had to leave the safety of the cave, their destination. Even now, he couldn't see the forest floor from the air.

Good.

The river caught his eye as they moved closer. Wide and deep, it would act as another barrier since the falls were on the other side.

He wouldn't be able to use much magic and remain undetected, even in an area Fae would naturally avoid. Xander couldn't ward the cave. A protection spell would be sensed immediately and defeat its purpose. He was even leery to try a spell such as the magical *stay out* his cousin had on the Faery Stones of Skye. It, too, could be sensed.

Janet gasped and crushed her eyes shut when Xander dove for a large boulder.

"Lass, the view is beautiful, if you would but look."

She shook her head, and he swallowed a laugh, lest he offend her.

"There's nothing to fear," he said into her ear as he touched down. "You can let go now, we're on the ground, so to speak."

The rush of the Falls must've caught Janet's attention, for she lifted her head from his chest, but she didn't leave his embrace.

Xander wasn't going to complain. He liked holding her.

He released her when she tugged at his arms, but she didn't move more than a few inches away. She favored her foot, and he frowned.

Xander needed to get them settled so he could take

a look at it.

"This place isn't ugly at all. It's beautiful." There was wonder in her voice as she looked up at the greater and lesser waterfalls.

The larger of the two curved inward, forming a wide asymmetrical half-circle. Below it was a pool, deep blue and serene. The water there was warm.

Down farther, moving away from the largest Falls, there were a series of tiny to medium-sized waterfalls in the rocky cliff faces. The water there, too, was warm.

He and Alana had explored the area extensively when they were wee.

Xander laughed, gripping Janet's arm when she wobbled on her feet. "Fae feel differently, because the foliage —"

"Is like home."

"Aye." He nodded, tipping her chin up to look into her face.

Her cheeks were flushed, and her lips parted.

His heart stuttered and desire warmed his limbs, especially where they touched. Xander would've kissed her, but she gently pulled away, looking down at the pool at the base of the larger waterfall, and then gesturing to the river.

"It's so warm here."

"Aye, the weather is usually like this. Not like the Human Realm. It's regulated by Fae mages who have weather magic."

Janet looked over her shoulder. "Really?"

Xander nodded. Their mating bond throbbed, and he wanted to reach for her. He cleared his throat. "They work together to keep things mild. Sunny days, warm nights, and only rain when we need it."

Silence fell as Janet took in their surroundings. Birds called to each other, and branches rustled as tree dwellers hopped from place to place. Insects chirped and trilled.

Serenity surrounded them and Xander breathed it in, calming completely despite their situation. Hopefully their environment would have the same effect on his wife. He couldn't sense what she was feeling exactly, but her form radiated agitation.

"What now?" Janet whispered.

"There's a cave behind the larger fall. We'll hide there."

"For how long?" She faced him, swallowing audibly.

Xander wanted to kiss her throat. Wipe that look off her face. "Until it's safe."

Her sapphire eyes misted over, and his stomach fluttered. "How long is tha'?"

Xander didn't want to tell her he hadn't a clue. He didn't know the watch schedule anymore. He didn't want to admit he was going to have to leave her to find out, either. He'd have to go back to the Faery Stones alone, discover the most vulnerable time for the guards, so he could open the Stones and get them back to the Human Realm.

They'd been lucky, in a way, when they'd arrived. There had only been three Fae Warriors instead of the usual six. Although now that they were there, his father would likely double or triple the guard at the king's behest.

All that discussion was for later. When they were safe.

Xander pulled her back into his arms, and she didn't fight him, nor did she question why he hadn't answered her. "Let's go into the cave."

Janet nodded and hid her face again, as he gathered her closer and pushed off the boulder.

He glided downward, toward the rushing falls.

They both gasped as he flew through the water. It was cold, a shock, and soaked them from head to toe, but it was the quickest way into the large cavern he and Alana had discovered as children.

They could've avoided getting wet if they'd scaled the cliff and slipped behind the water, but Janet couldn't have even if she wasn't injured.

The place was dark, and she shivered as soon as he landed. She broke their physical contact, but once again didn't go far.

Xander pumped his wings to discard excess water and ran his hands through his short hair. "We can stay here for the night. We should be safe enough." The roar of the waterfall behind them rivaled the one in his ears.

His bond with Janet tugged at him. He couldn't sense anything but uncertainty from her, but it didn't chase away his lust. The stronger magic of the realm made him want her more.

Every time they touched; his body thrummed. Being alone with her was going to complicate things if Xander couldn't keep his hands to himself. Even now, he was compelled to reach for her again, to touch even her hand.

Holding her close while they'd flown high above the clouds had fired him in more than one way. He'd wanted to whip up her skirts and slip inside her, take her while his wings pumped hard. Make her his —

"Xander."

Her whisper jolted him, made his cock twitch, too, but one look at the fright in her wide sapphire eyes, the pallor on her gorgeous face, dissipated his joy over his magic and deflated his desire.

She was even more alarmed than she'd been moments before as they'd arrived at Grànnda Falls. It was probably the darkness of their new surroundings.

His heart fluttered and he wanted to make her feel better.

Nay.

Xander *needed* her to feel better.

He rested his hands on her shoulders and ignored the energy that zinged up his arms from the contact. "Lass, we're going to be fine."

"I want ta go home."

"I know. I'll get us home." He flexed his wings.

"When?" Her teeth chattered.

"When 'tis safe."

Xander drew her into his chest again and like before, she didn't fight him, but Janet didn't wrap her arms around him, either.

"When is that?" her whisper was muffled against his wet leine.

He still couldn't tell her of his uncertainty, despite her prodding. Janet wouldn't like him having to leave her, his gut shouted.

They'd have to be smart. Stealthy. Despite Xander's reveling in the return of his powers—his wings—it was going to take his wits—*their* wits—to get them back to the Human Realm.

He shifted Janet closer, and she hissed. "Lass?"

"Sorry." She tried to mask the wince on her pretty face but couldn't. "My…my ankle still hurts."

"That I can do something about. I can also make this place light and warm."

She offered a small smile, and it took all he was made of not to kiss her.

Xander had stolen one kiss before he'd flown away from the Faery Stones, but Janet hadn't kissed him back, although she'd not protested either.

He'd told Duncan he'd no worries about his sister's virtue, but Xander wasn't a fool. The magic— and their bond—would drive them toward sealing their fate the more time they spent together.

If the lass didn't turn him away, he would take her. He didn't have the control otherwise. Besides, he couldn't afford to become ill if they didn't consummate their bond.

He wasn't a brute; he would leave things up to Janet, but he didn't know how much time they had. He needed his magic for them to survive. To get home.

Home?

Since when had Xander started thinking of the Human Realm—Dunvegan—as home?

"What can ye do abou' my ankle?" Her voice pulled him from his thoughts.

"I'm not a healer, but I know a few spells. I can try."

"Magic?"

"Aye."

Her expression held dread and curiosity.

"We're in the Realm of the Fae, my lady. Magic is our reality."

Janet shivered against him.

Xander held her tighter. "I won't hurt you."

Her blue eyes burned his face. "I ken it. I trust ye." Janet's simple, sure words made his heart flip.

She *trusted* him.

"First, let me get some lights."

"How?"

"You'll see." Xander kissed her forehead. Once again, he couldn't help himself. Her small smile in response was all the encouragement he needed.

He backed up and sucked in a breath, spreading his arms out, palms raised flat. Xander pictured one of the many storerooms in the vast palace. He'd have to be quick and pray no one was *in* the room to see the magic orbs disappear when he called them forth.

Xander felt Janet's eyes on him even as his own remained closed. He concentrated and whispered the spellwords. It took a few tries, but when he pushed more power behind the phrase, he felt the magic move within him. Sweat trickled down his temple, but within moments, his palms were filled with two glowing globes.

Janet gasped.

He opened his eyes and met her gaze, smiling at the wonder in her expression. "I'm out of practice. That took longer — and more power — than it should've."

"Wh-what are they?" She reached out, before pulling her hand back.

"They're lights. You can touch them; they shan't burn. If they're not bright enough, you tell them to alight more, but the spell will burn out faster."

"Then wha'?"

"Then I'd have to recharge them."

He called forth six more lights. Using magic exhausted Xander, but he had enough energy left to order the orbs to perch themselves along the cavern walls. They stuck and would remain there until he removed them.

Janet stared, not saying much; he preferred her fascination to horror over magic.

Their bond was already deepening.

Xander could almost sense her emotions. If he concentrated enough to see the golden rope of the mating bond itself, he could even see the aura it displayed. The glow was currently pastel colors, a mixture of both of their current feelings. They were tired, but calm.

However, his mate sat on a rock, shivering in her wet clothing.

"Lass, I shall call forth a bed; you should get out of those clothes."

In the newly lit cavern, her cheeks went crimson. "Nay, I've nothing ta wear."

Xander whipped his tunic over his head. "I can light a fire, but you can't sit in wet fabric."

"But—"

"You've nothing to fash about." He strode over, squatted in front of her and started unlacing her bodice. "The sun will dry our clothes. We can lay them on the rocks."

Janet stared. She swallowed.

Xander resisted the urge to lay a line of kisses down her neck and throat. When her corset loosened enough to bare the leine beneath, and hinted at her breasts, he tore his eyes away. It was ivory in color and would be see-through.

It was a temptation he couldn't resist, despite the chemise under it.

He forced himself to straighten and reached for the ties on his trews.

She still hadn't moved from the rock she'd made into a seat, but she did move her hands to catch her untied bodice, cover her body. Janet looked up at him, her cheeks adorably pink.

"What is it?"

"N-n-nothin'." Her words belied her eyes, which were skimming his naked chest.

Awareness prickled between them, and Xander gave into a smile.

Janet was studying him, as if pleased with what she saw.

If she watched him like that much longer, his body would respond. Arousal rode beneath the surface, and Xander had to bite back a groan. He cleared his throat. "Give me your skirts, your corset, and I will lay them out, so you don't have to walk."

"As…as ye wish."

He paused as she said the phrase he often uttered.

"Can…can ye please turn 'round?"

"Aye." He complied, imagining his mate undressing.

Xander tried to ignore the blood pounding in his ears, thrumming through his limbs. Heat settled in his lower belly, and his cock started to harden. His wings twitched. He forced his wet leather trews off one hip, then the other, wishing he could remove the short pants he wore beneath. It would be too much for his mate. Fae had no qualms about nudity, but humans certainly did.

"Here." Janet averted her gaze when he whirled her way again.

Gathering the heavy wet wool into his arms, Xander ordered himself not to study her barely covered skin. Her chemise was white, and also wet, but Janet had pulled it away from her body. It was no longer clinging.

Unfortunately.

She wouldn't meet his eyes.

Xander smiled to himself. Janet MacLeod was appealing, with her mix of strength and vulnerability. He wanted her even more.

Her face was crimson, her dark locks damp and mussed.

Their bond was palpable, desire and mixed emotions bouncing between the two of them, making him fight tremors. Xander needed some air.

He grabbed their boots and forced one foot in front of the other, moving away from Janet. The water roared as he got closer to the falls, but he was able to stay dry as he slipped away from the cave's wide mouth, staying on the thick ledge of the cliff face beside it.

Xander put their clothes where the sun beat down, but as low as he could manage, so if someone flew overhead the garments would remain unseen. He probably could've used a spell to dry them, but he wanted to steal a proper bed for them to sleep on.

Something that large would exhaust him even more, so he needed to conserve his energy. He also wanted to try to heal her ankle.

Janet still wouldn't look at him when he slid back inside. She sat on the same small boulder, her knees to her chest and her arms around them. Her face was buried on top of them, and she rocked slightly.

He wanted to banish the uncertainty he felt from her.

Xander craved her smile, even her touch. He took a seat beside her, but she didn't react. He tried to ignore the slight bite of rejection. "Lass?"

Wide blue eyes met his gaze, but she looked so scared it made his heart thump.

Xander reached for her hand and squeezed. "You're cold." He wanted to rub her arms, pull her against him again, but didn't. "I'll get you a bed, then light a fire and see if I can fix your foot."

chapter nine

he didn't miss her intake of breath when he gripped her foot; although it was as gentle as he could manage.

Xander's gaze followed the curve of her shapely calf up to her knee.

Janet's ankle was delicate, her skin pale and creamy, and he wanted to touch her, caress every smooth line. She was tall for a female, and seeing her bare legs made him want more. She was utterly feminine. Her chemise was thin, but it pooled between her legs, hiding the part of her body he wanted to see most.

His cock strained against his short pants; despite his assurance it was *not* the time. His wife was injured; he was supposed to be healing her, not seducing her. Besides, there was nothing even remotely sexual about his touch.

When Xander looked up, he could see their mating bond. It glowed gold, wrapping around them both, disappearing into her chest. He looked down and saw the same on his body. The aura he'd sensed earlier was still there; his emotions and hers. It had a red pulse.

Janet's foot hurt her.

He frowned. If his touch was causing her pain, she said nothing.

She reached out, as if to caress the mating bond.

Tingles shot down his spine, and his wings flexed of their own accord.

Janet gasped.

"You can see the bond," Xander said.

"Aye. I...touched it."

"I felt it."

"Me too." Janet swallowed, her eyes locking onto his face. "It's odd..."

Xander nodded. "It will deepen with time. You will start to sense my feelings, and I will be able to sense yours. The lore says we'll be able to think and feel as one, even communicate by thoughts."

She didn't say anything, so he let the magic information drop. If Janet asked, he'd tell her all she wanted to know of the ring and mating bonds.

Now, it was overwhelming. Instinct and their bond told him as much. Janet might know of magic because of Alana and Angus, but it was different to experience it.

He rotated her foot and she winced, gripping the blanket beneath her.

Xander had lifted her onto the mattress as soon as he'd conjured it. He'd taken it from a guest room he'd been in once in the palace. Hopefully its disappearance went unnoticed. It'd taken all his willpower not to lay her down and settle on top of her. "I'm sorry. I didn't mean to hurt you. I just wanted to make sure it's not broken."

"I'm hale." The words were strained, but his lass didn't cry out.

By the Goddess, she's strong.

Beautiful.

Mine.

Xander caressed her ankle, then closed his eyes, calling magic to him. "Won't be long now." He whispered spellwords.

His hands were warm, and even though his touch wasn't inappropriate, Janet's stomach flipped. "Okay," she forced the answer out, borrowing a word she'd learned from Claire. Her sister-by-marriage said the affirmative a great deal.

Xander's hands started to glow.

Janet watched, fascinated as his skin brightened, lighting from the inside out. Like the magic lanterns he'd *borrowed*.

He caressed her ankle, her foot, and even her calf.

Warmth spread up her leg, but then it kept going, heating her belly, her chest, her arms. Her heart picked up speed and her cheeks burned.

The place between her legs started to throb and she wanted to squeeze her thighs to make it stop, but her fated husband was still chanting words she didn't understand.

Janet started to pant and imagined his hands moving higher on her body. His fingers teasing, feather-light touches all over her form.

Her breasts felt heavy, her nipples hard and achy. She swallowed a moan. Wanted to lean back into the soft mattress he'd called from the palace.

Touch me. The words played on the tip of her tongue, but she couldn't muster the courage to say them.

Pain faded from her foot, but she was so distracted by the desire consuming her, Janet couldn't tell if whatever magic Xander was using was the cause.

If he didn't get on with—

"There. Better?" He looked up. When their gazes collided, his violet eyes went wide, and his nostrils flared.

Janet moaned.

What's wrong with me?

Xander's fingertips slipped from her foot, and he scooted backwards on the rough floor of the cave. The apple of his throat bobbed. "Lass..." The word was a croak.

Her eyes trailed his form, and she didn't miss the tented linen at his crotch. Thin fabric that could be gone in seconds. The arousal she'd felt against her stomach when he kissed her on the beach was before her now. Her desire had fed his, through their bond, no doubt.

Some of the haziness clouding her brain faded

now that they weren't touching, and embarrassment settled over Janet. She tore her gaze from his body, heat creeping up her neck. Different from the warmth of passion, this left her mortified that she'd stared at a half-naked man, even if he was supposed to be her mate.

"What type of a word is *mate* for people, anaway?" she blurted. Janet still couldn't look at him.

When Xander had shed his tunic, she'd caught herself staring. From all the recent times in his arms, against that chest, she'd felt his hard muscles. However, to see their beauty…

The Fae man was gorgeous. His chest was hairless, but Alana had told her Fae didn't have any body hair. Xander was broad and defined, with a tapered waist and many lines she wanted to explore.

Trace.

Kiss?

Janet cleared her throat. She'd seen tons of shirtless clansmen. Even MacLeods she had no blood tie to. Never had she been tempted, to…touch…kiss any of them. Nor had she been attracted to any of them in a physical way.

Is this magic?

Our bond?

"*Mate* is an old term, of course."

His words jolted her, and she fidgeted on the soft mattress. "We dinnae be animals."

Xander's deep chuckle appealed as much as he

did, and she looked at him. Couldn't help herself. The smile that curved his full mouth made her heart miss a beat.

Janet hadn't seen him smile much over the time she'd known him, but his smile was as gorgeous as he was.

"Nay. We're not. Fae use the same terms as humans. Husband, wife. But *mate* has hung on when it comes to these rare fated situations." He gestured between them. Xander stood from the rocky ground and went to retrieve the satchel he'd brought.

She watched as if transfixed, not able to muster a retort about fate. She studied the play of his muscles, how his iridescent wings caught the light of the globes he'd positioned around the cavern.

He was graceful in every movement.

Bonnie.

She still could say nothing as he returned to sit on the rock she'd perched on before.

His biceps contracted and released as he pulled on the bag's ties.

Janet stopped herself from asking him to come closer. Sit on the soft bedding next to her, as she reclined and relaxed.

"Hungry, lass?"

She jumped. Her stomach rumbled as if to answer for her. "Aye." Janet forced the word out. Had to say *something*, lest he think she'd gone mute…or daft.

If Xander was aware of her perusal and what his

nearly nude form was doing to her, his smile didn't give anything away.

Heat scorched her cheeks again. If she didn't get herself in order, being around this Fae man was likely to make her blush permanent.

Janet could feel their bond. His heartbeat echoed hers, like before. It was becoming as normal as breathing to have him close, either magically or physically. She chided herself for craving more.

"I have to go to the Faery Stones." His words were casual, and Xander leaned closer, handing her a chunk of bread with a strip of dried meat. "Alone."

Her yearning for him scattered her focus suddenly switching to panic. Not even his touch helped as their hands brushed in the transfer of food. "Nay…"

Xander paused. He squatted in front of her. "I must." His voice was low, serious, and the regret in his violet eyes was clear.

"Dinnae leave me." The statement was a plea, and normally it would have embarrassed her to utter such, but Janet was trying to stave off the panic at the idea of him going anywhere without her, even for a few moments.

He slid onto the mattress next to her, setting the food down on the cloth it'd been wrapped in. Xander tucked a strand of her damp hair behind her ear. "I shall wait until night falls. I'll be quick and be back before you can miss me."

Nay. I'd miss you immediately.

"I'll go wit' ye."

"Nay, lass. 'Tis too dangerous. I must determine *when* the guard is weak. So, we can get home."

Janet wanted to burrow into his chest.

"You'll know where I am. You'll feel our bond." Xander took her hand and squeezed.

When she glanced down, she noticed her slice of bread was now in crumbs on her lap. She'd crushed it without realizing.

"I'll return to you. You've my word."

A vow.

It didn't make her feel better. Janet swallowed, her mouth suddenly dry, and her hunger had vanished. Her stomach was a ball of nerves.

"Eat, I need you strong. As soon as the sun is down, I shall go. Then you can bathe, if you wish it."

"Bathe?"

Xander nodded, a smile playing at his lips. "There's a pool at the back of this cavern. It's waist deep and naturally warm. This whole area is riddled with hot springs. The water is pure and soothing."

"Ye've been here a'fore?"

"Aye. Alana and I discovered this cave years ago. My cousin was always too curious for her own good." He laughed and it made Janet's stomach flutter. "Was she not, she would've never met your brother, but that's a story for another time." The fondness in his voice made her want to frown.

She adored both her sisters-by-marriage.

However…Janet wanted Xander to speak of her with such feeling. Or…more.

Is that magic, too?

She shivered.

Was she jealous of the former princess because Xander cared for her?

Perhaps a little, if she was honest.

"I had a particularly bad day, and my cousin wanted to make me feel better, actually. So, we went exploring. Alana wanted to know why most Fae despise this place. We found the cave and the hot springs."

Janet couldn't look away. Xander had never spoken of himself in her presence, and she craved to hear something of his past. Of his childhood. "What happened?" she whispered.

One look told her he'd understood that she hadn't referred to the discovery of the cave, but what had happened to cause his horrible day.

His eyes clouded, as if he had just realized what he'd said. Xander averted his gaze. "Just eat. No reason to drudge up old memories."

She reached for him. Janet couldn't help it. Their gazes collided when she covered his hand with hers. Her heart jumped at the contact. "Please tell me. I want ta hear abou' ye."

The apple of his throat bobbed, but he nodded. However, he looked away again. Wouldn't meet her eyes, even when she tugged on his wrist.

He's embarrassed.

Janet scooted closer to Xander, the food on her lap forgotten.

"My mother was a Fae princess. The king never forgave his sister for sneaking off and marrying my father, the *winged* captain of his guard. It *broke* her, especially since King Fillan forgave my father before I was born. I didn't see much of her as a lad. She turned to smoking Acana root when I was wee, so when I did see her, most of the time she was in a haze. Not sure she even knew it was me, her son."

"What's Acana root?"

"Remember the maroon-barked trees?"

"Aye." Janet entwined her fingers with his.

Xander's pale locks dropped over his eyes, and she wanted to tilt his face up, brush his hair off his forehead, but she kept her hands to herself.

She could see the mating bond, but there was a blue glow hovering above the golden radiance of it. She felt odd, like a weight rested on her chest.

Xander's sadness.

I can feel *it.*

Janet moved even closer, until her shoulder brushed his chest. She wanted to throw her arms around him but didn't. His bare skin against the sleeve of her chemise would have to be enough for now.

"The Acana tree has healing properties. When used properly it aids healing magic as a sedative, but it's abused all over the realm. Addicts crush it, ingest, or snort it, or even smoke it. My mother was a healer of some renown, before she was mired by her selfishness." Now Xander's voice was bitter.

She hung on every word.

"I was about four and ten. So proud of myself because I'd mastered the obstacle course faster than any of my training mates. Even my father was proud of me. He'd *said* so. The first praise in longer than I could remember. I rushed to my mother's rooms; I had to tell her. I found her on the floor. *Unconscious.* Close to death, actually. I called the healers. They arrived with my father. He kept muttering how Acana root addiction was weak and dishonored him. I made a vow never to dishonor him that day. I didn't want him to look at *me* like that. Alana took me away afterward. As she often did after an *experience* with either of my parents."

Janet's heart ached. She could feel his mixed emotions toward both his parents, as well as his overwhelming regret. Her vision blurred. "Xander."

He laughed, but it had a bitter edge. If he'd heard her whisper his name, he didn't acknowledge it. "I dishonored him anyway, following Alana to the Realm of the Humans...cutting off my warrior braid."

"Xander."

Her fated husband finally met her eyes. His expression shifted from angry to concerned. "Oh, lass, don't shed tears for me."

Janet leaned in, pressing her lips to his.

Xander wrapped his arms around her and pulled her closer, meeting her kiss.

She groaned when he invaded her mouth but pushed her tongue to his instead of pulling away. Her breasts flattened to his chest, and she snaked her arms around his neck.

He kissed her until she melted into him.

Heat spread all over Janet's body, settling low in her belly. Her core throbbed and pulsed, every sensation more excruciating than when he'd healed her ankle.

Her chemise was mostly dry now, but the light fabric was encumbering, weighty, and made it hard to breathe. She panted against him, clutching at his bare shoulders.

"Lass, you make me lose control." Xander's voice was thicker, deeper than normal. He rested his forehead against hers. His breathing was rough, and his chest heaved against hers.

"I'm sorry," Janet whispered.

He lifted his head, placing his hands on her shoulders. "Don't be."

Even the smirk he wore was beautiful, and it did funny things to her already overheated insides.

"Are you innocent?" he asked.

Fire licked her face for a different reason than his mouth moving over hers. "Aye."

Xander nodded, the look in his violet eyes so tender, Janet wanted to melt all over again. "I'd assumed so."

"I dinnae please you?" She looked down. If he said she was too forward, or worse, didn't make him feel what he made *her* feel, Janet didn't know what she would do.

The idea...*hurt.*

When he chuckled, her stomach somersaulted.

"Aye, you please me. I was going to apologize for being so rough."

"Oh." It took all she was made of not too look away again. "Ye dinnae be rough."

Xander smiled and hugged her close.

Janet closed her eyes against his shoulder, her whole body still thrumming. "I'm sorry abou' yer mother."

"Thank you," Xander whispered. "Sorry to make you sad..."

"You dinnae I mean, I was hurtin' *for* you," she whispered.

"I know. I could feel it. Our bond is deepening." He smiled, and it was full of that same tenderness. He still held her.

So much heat and promise.

Janet trembled against his warmth. "Already?"

"Aye, it seems so."

Her heart flipped.

Is it wrong to hope for more?

She'd been so determined that magic wouldn't decide this for her.

Had something changed?

Janet ignored the questions she was too afraid to answer. She buried her face against Xander's chest, letting him hold her, reveling in his body, his warmth.

He'd keep her safe, get her home.

She'd worry about the rest later.

chapter ten

leaving her was harder than he'd imagined. His body was tight, and Xander was shaking all over; even his wings trembled of their own accord.

If he closed his eyes, all he could see were her sapphire ones.

So much trust.

He swallowed and squared his shoulders, wishing he could cover Janet and the cave area in a protection spell.

"Damn it all," Xander whispered, clutching his fists at his sides. He pushed off the ledge outside the cave, pumping his wings.

They ached from disuse, but he ignored the discomfort and rose higher into the night, whispering a masking spell that would leave him undetectable to *most* Fae Warriors.

Xander added his invisibility spell, praying to the Goddess he'd get the information he needed and return to his mate unscathed — and quickly, as he'd promised her.

If King Fillan had Fae mages and wizards scrying for them, at least Janet would be safe in the cave. The mating bond shouldn't contain discernable magic on its own, so even without a protection spell, she was likely hidden enough. Although her human blood would be sensed if they searched hard. That he could do nothing about, except pray the mating bond disguised her in some way. Alana had been right to doubt that when he'd mentioned it, but he could pray, could he not?

Both his spells would be detectable by any mage worth his or her salt—as all mages and wizards in the king's menagerie were.

Nay. I cannot despair.

Xander blocked worry and the danger enshrouding him. He'd been in risky, even dire, situations before. He would endure and do what he needed to do to protect Janet.

I have no choice.

He'd made vows to his fated wife, as well as his cousin.

Promises he *would* keep.

Xander had waited until she'd fallen asleep to leave their cavern.

The day had fatigued them both, so he hadn't had long to wait. When Janet's belly was full of the meat and bread he'd brought, his lovely bride had fallen asleep in his arms.

He'd lain her on the plush Fae bed and kissed her softly. His chest had ached as he'd forced one booted foot in front of the other on the way out of the cavern.

Knowledge was the only thing that would get them home safely, but leaving her vulnerable when she had no magic was almost as bad as taking her with him.

Nay.

His gut told him he was doing the right thing. If he had to fight when he got to the Faery Stones, she'd be in more danger than at the Falls. There was also that part of him that still didn't want her to witness him at battle again, possibly killing.

Xander didn't want to kill any Fae Warriors, his former brothers, but he would do what he needed to do to survive.

For Janet and himself.

He, too, was tired, and Xander fought the exhaustion threatening as he flew back to the forest and grassy knoll his people called the Field of Light.

An idea bloomed as he soared on a thermal like he had earlier in the day. He spread his arms and sucked clean warm air into his lungs. It was refreshing, despite his dark thoughts.

If he was forced to kill whatever guard was present at the Faery Stones, perhaps the king would think he'd done so to escape.

It could gain us some time.

Torches were visible as he neared the area, but the soft breeze had no effect on the source of light, as they were the same magic globes he'd called into the cave.

The Faery Stones rested dormant on their platform. A large Acana tree was rooted not ten feet from the place and hung tall overhead, partially obscuring his view. Branches with their pale pink leaves swayed in the warm night air.

Xander slowed his hard pace, landing not far from the dais, on the same side he'd pulled Janet to her feet and into his arms.

Voices carried, but he couldn't make anything specific out.

A bonfire was lit, making a wide section of the terrain like daylight.

His father had doubled the guard.

Twelve winged Fae Warriors.

Four on the dais, standing at attention on opposite sides of the Faery Stones.

Three on the ground, close enough to touch the dais.

Two more patrolled the perimeter, marching side by side, boots cutting through the orange and blue grass.

The other three either stood or marched further out in the Field of Light.

Xander didn't recognize all of them, but he did spot Mikhias and Ruark as the closest patrolling pair. Neither of his former brethren he'd battled with that morning looked worse for the wear.

He muttered his invisibility spell again just for good measure, although none of the Fae Warriors seemed to notice his presence.

Good.

Being able to fight well didn't necessarily mean they were gifted with much magic, which was to

Xander's favor. If he could watch them interact, perhaps hear them talk, he wouldn't have to snatch one and compel answers out of him.

"Ye should've killed the traitor when ye had the chance," Ruark barked at Mikhias as they circled the dais. The redheaded warrior scowled at his companion. The Warrior's inflection revealed his low caste.

"You could've done so yourself, just as well," Mikhias returned, narrowing his eyes. He shoved his long dark plait over his shoulder, then rested a hand on the hilt of his sword.

"Ye know as well as I the blast spell was unexpected."

Xander straightened his back, fighting his instinct to duck behind the dais as they looped around, passing within several feet of him. They couldn't see him. He needed to trust his spell.

Besides, invisibility didn't always mean they couldn't *hear* him. Sometimes a keen ear could sense what was concealed by magic.

Ruark gave the Warriors on the ground a nod, and the one on the right—a fair-haired winged soldier Xander didn't know—returned the gesture.

"'Tis yer fault we're stuck out here at all hours," Ruark growled. "Circlin' as if we're fledglings on our first tour." Humiliation saturated his voice.

Mikhias's answer was unintelligible as the pair's foot patrol went wide, but Xander had heard both the king's and his father's names in the sentence, as well as a few Fae curses. He strained his ears but could catch nothing more.

Bollocks.

Then again, the two were griping, not really sharing any pertinent information.

Ruark had been in his training classes as a lad, as they were of an age, and Xander had never cared for the impulsive Fae man. However, his younger friend Mikhias was the more dangerous of the two. Rumors among the castle guard said he had a heavy hand with servants and a reputation as rapist to any woman who dared tell him nay.

Xander had always been curious as to how much truth lay in those rumors because the king might be ruthless, but he did not abide women abusers or rapists. It was a punishable offense.

Unless his victims were too afraid to turn him in. Unlike Ruark, Mikhias was higher born.

Xander frowned. He'd never been witness to anything untoward, since he'd served his duties at Alana's side, as her personal bodyguard, but he'd never been fond of womanizers or abusers.

Female Fae were usually amenable to a man who approached her in the correct manner, so it wasn't necessary. It wasn't uncommon for most Fae—of any class or caste—to take several lovers before marrying.

Once a Fae was wed—fated or chosen— monogamy was expected, unless both parties were open to a third—or more—lover sharing the marriage bed.

Not in my *marriage bed.*

He'd never been possessive, but the idea of another man — Fae or human — touching Janet made Xander want to stab something.

No one else will touch her.

Ever.

He shook his head. Needed to focus on the task at hand, keep his thoughts off his lass for now. He'd return to her side soon enough. Hopefully she'd be asleep and none the wiser. Xander hadn't liked the panic in those blue eyes.

Silently drawing his sword, he studied the Warriors on the dais, then the three standing guard on the ground. The others were all far enough away, but he couldn't snatch one inconspicuously, nor were they standing close enough for a stunning spell to take them all out at once.

If one fell, the others would obviously notice. He couldn't let his drive for information override his caution.

I cannot get captured.

Janet would have no chance without him.

Xander reached magically, seeking the mating bond. Her heartbeat was calm, echoing his like it had since the moment their souls had been woven together.

The even rhythm was in his mind, as if he now had two pulses. It'd only been a day, but it was *normal* already. As normal as the air moving in and out of his lungs.

Almost as if he couldn't remember before their first kiss on the beach.

Xander had always been able to read minds, inadvertently invading people's privacy. Most Fae automatically shielded their thoughts, as the trait was not uncommon, but humans could not.

Living in the Human Realm had been a form of torture; he was never alone, not even in his own head, unless Alana helped him.

Janet being joined with him, his complete awareness of her; it made him crave more. A deeper connection.

Which should scare the shite out of him but didn't.

Xander could sense her breathing. It was even and deep.

Sleeping indeed.

Good.

A shout went up, snapping him to attention. He gripped his sword tighter and silently inched around to the front of the dais, just as two of the soldiers that'd been in the Field of Light's perimeter dashed over, one waving his arms and his wings alike. He had brown hair, his warrior braid thick and long. "We've been summoned!"

"Summoned?" The Fae Warrior on the ground at the far end of the dais joined them, flexing his wings and frowning. "The king himself told Gannon and me to remain here."

The fair-haired one who'd acknowledged Ruark earlier nodded. "Aye, 'twas our orders."

Xander moved closer. Now he stood with them, as if he would take part in their conversation. He prayed to the Goddess and Janet's God alike that no one would sense his spell.

"Captain Daegus ordered our return."

He startled at his father's name. Gripped his sword tighter.

"Mikhias and Ruark are to remain. We are to go." The Warrior's voice carried, and the four winged soldiers on the dais glided down to the ground.

"Were the traitor and the human lass found?" one asked.

"I know not," the brown-haired Warrior answered.

Sweat broke out on Xander's forehead. He inspected the mating bond, but Janet's heart rate hadn't changed.

"What do the mages say?" another Warrior asked.

"I was not told."

Mikhias and Ruark made their way to the group now. Both wore scowls.

"The captain has summoned?" Ruark demanded.

"Aye, we're to report immediately."

"No' ye two, though." The one called Gannon smirked.

Mikhias glared and jolted forward, but Ruark grabbed his upper arm.

Gannon chuckled. "The favored one is no longer such."

Favored one?

"We must go. Captain Daegus does no' like to repeat orders," a Warrior urged.

Nay, he does not.

His father wasn't above punishment if he even *perceived* disobedience. Xander stood next to the two glowering Fae Warriors, watching the ten other winged soldiers fall into line, the one who'd received the summons in the front position of leader. They pumped their wings simultaneously and rose as a unit, as they'd been trained, despite their two wingmates missing from the formation.

Mikhias and Ruark looked at each other.

Well, *glared* was more accurate.

Xander smirked. He was no empath, but blame was written all over the two warriors that'd been left behind.

They started to argue even before the rest of their Wing was out of sight.

"When I catch that traitor, I'm going to rip his wings off," Mikhias barked.

"Aye, I'm sure," Ruark scoffed, tossing his auburn braid over his shoulder.

His companion growled but said nothing.

Xander studied them.

They were distracted, but was staying here going to be helpful?

He couldn't compel them without becoming visible.

They were angry enough at each other to let information slip, weren't they?

Perhaps they knew nothing, since his father and the king were not pleased with them.

Xander longed to return to his wife's side, but he was at the Faery Stones with a suddenly light guard; he needed to take advantage of what he could.

Staring at the sword in his hands, he weighed his options. He'd overtaken these two just that morning.

Could he do it again?

Perhaps even retrieve Janet and try to get them home?

Nay.

His gut said it wasn't worth the risk. Xander needed to know why his father called back the other warriors.

Ruark pumped his wings and rose to prop himself on the edge of the dais, foregoing the stairs that were closer.

"What're you doing?" Mikhias demanded.

"Xander-the-traitor is far from here. Never liked 'im much, but the Warrior isnae a fool. If I'm stuck here, migh' as well make tha best of it." The redheaded winged soldier dug in his pocket and pulled out a silver flask.

"You're the fool. Even he knows *when* he's found, he's dead. The Stones are his only way out of this realm.

He's probably watching."

Xander's heart sped up and he gripped his sword tighter. The Faery Stones were warded against stealth magic, but the area around them was not.

Can he sense me? Is this a trap?

Ruark took a swig of whatever contraband he had in the flask. He scoffed when he looked at his companion. "The lass is human. He's hidden her away. He'll no' be here tonight. Xander-the-traitor is lower than the lowest dog now. Captain Daegus himself has disavowed their blood ties and agreed with the king's order to put him to death."

Ice slid over Xander's wings and down his spine. His *father* would do the deed himself?

He swallowed against the sudden lump in his throat.

"Aye. Blood ties won't save the traitor." Mikhias nodded.

"Aye." Ruark echoed the gesture. "Why would he come back here?"

"*That* 'tis the question they all want answered." The dark-haired Warrior thumbed over his shoulder in the general direction of the palace.

"And who is the lass?" Ruark mused.

Xander narrowed his eyes, growling. He wanted to demand they leave his mate out of their speculations.

Mikhias froze.

"What is it?" Ruark asked, squaring his shoulders. His wings flexed, catching the magic lanterns. Colors of the rainbow danced across the span of his iridescent wing-skin, but Xander tore his eyes away, staring at Mikhias.

"Did you hear something?"

Bollocks.

"Nay. Did ye?"

"Aye. We're not alone."

Ruark hopped off the dais, scanning the area. "Yer bein' paranoid, my friend." He pocketed his flask.

"Nay." Mikhias shook his head and drew his sword. He shouted a Fae spellword.

Xander cursed.

His magic was nullified.

They saw him at the same time.

"Traitor," Mikhias spat.

"Ye were right," Ruark breathed, drawing his sword.

Xander squared his shoulders, bracing himself for impact—magical or physical.

"Good, perhaps he'll answer questions before we turn him in." Mikhias narrowed his eyes, inching forward.

Both Fae Warriors advanced as if they were going to circle him.

"Nay," Xander said.

"Nay?" Ruark barked, arching one auburn brow. His overconfidence rolled off him in waves.

"I won't be answering questions tonight. But you will." Xander called a ball of light to his palm and flung it at them.

Mikhias dove for the ground, but the stunning spell hit Ruark in the chest and he crumpled to the orange and blue grass.

Xander slid backwards, brandishing his sword at the dark-haired Warrior, chanting the words of the strongest compelling spell he knew. Alana had taught him years ago.

Mikhias froze as soon as he made it to his feet.

"Stop!" Xander shouted. He glanced at Ruark to make sure he was still unconscious, but regardless, he hadn't much time. He strode to Mikhias, staring into his eyes. "Sheath your sword."

The Warrior didn't hesitate, as if his captain stood before him with orders. He shoved his large weapon into its scabbard, squaring his shoulders, awaiting the next command.

Xander smiled, locking his gaze onto Mikhias's pale blue eyes. "Now, Sir Mikhias. You will tell me what I need to know."

chapter eleven

anet awoke shivering. She reached for the blanket, to pull it higher over her body, but paused at the unfamiliar feel beneath her fingertips. It wasn't the large MacLeod plaid she always had on her bed.

Too soft. Not wool.

"Where am I?" She blinked, staring up at a wide natural—rocky?—ceiling. She could hear the rush of thick water.

Everything came whooshing back, so fast it made her head spin and stole her breath. Janet shot to a sitting position, trembling from the chill in the air.

A cave.

Grànnda Falls.

The Fae Realm.

"Dinnae be home. Dinnae be a' Dunvegan."

Also….she was alone.

"Xander," Janet breathed. She tried again, this time louder.

Still no answer, even when she shouted his name.

He was gone. Must've gone to the Faery Stones, as he said he'd have to.

She sucked in a breath and closed her eyes. Janet could feel the mating bond. His heartbeat still echoed hers.

That means he's well, right?

Tremors danced across her frame, and she clutched the soft Fae blankets. Janet was cold, and not from temperature alone. The air was moist and humid not exactly frigid, but it wasn't overly warm either.

The cavern was dim. Her gaze darted around the walls. Xander's orbs still surrounded her, but they were a much softer glow than before. As if he'd blown out candles so she could sleep.

"*Soillsich,*" Janet commanded, as he'd taught her. The word meant *alight,* in Gaelic and Fae, and Xander had explained the simple term would make the globes brighten.

Immediately the place lit up, all the orbs as radiant as before. As if the cave was filled with daylight.

It made her feel better. She smiled, looking around the wide space. Her first magic spell and it'd *worked.* "Shame Xander missed it."

Angus, too. Her nephew would've been delighted.

Would she be able to perform magic when they got home?

Or was it the realm?

Magic was *alive* here, as Xander had told her.

Even with its rocky walls and dirty floor, the cavern looked almost friendly when lit up. Not a home, but not as foreboding as in the dark.

Janet's eye caught the small pool in the right rear corner, just like her fated husband had said. She shivered as damp air hit her face.

Xander had said the water in the pool was naturally heated because of a hot spring.

She could bathe. Get warm. Not have to be concerned about being nude with her winged Warrior in the cavern.

It was likely the only privacy she'd have until they returned to Skye.

Her skirts, leine and corset rested — folded — on the small boulder they'd both used for a seat. Janet was touched that he would've taken such care with her garments. He must've brought them inside before he'd left.

I can get dressed.

She'd have to use a blanket to dry off though. Janet gathered the softer of the two bed coverings into her arms and headed to the pool. She halved the blanket and laid it next to the small body of water.

Squatting, she dipped her hand into the spring. Xander had been right. Steam rose idly into the air, as if she'd boiled pots of water over a fire.

Inviting.

Janet smiled and stood, discarding her chemise. She folded it and rested the thin underdress next to the blanket. The chill in the damp air bit at her naked skin, so she wasted no time getting in the water. She stepped into the pool, sighing as the warm liquid caressed her legs. It came to her knees, and she wanted to submerge her body, but wasn't fond of the idea that rocks might scrape her.

She ran her hand along the side of the spring. It was smooth, as if carved. Gingerly, Janet sat, leaning against the heated rock, as if she was in the wooden tub at home.

Xander had said the hot springs were natural, but this pool felt sculpted. It must be old, and the water must have smoothed out the rock's surface over time.

Like the pebbles her nephew always gathered on the beach. He collected the softest ones. Angus liked colored rocks the best.

"Home," Janet whispered.

Her Fae Warrior would get her home. She had no worries about not seeing her family again. Janet and Xander would be home as soon as it was safe to open the Faery Stones.

Maybe on the morrow?

She banished all negativity, slipping even farther into the water, letting the heat of the swirling pool seep into her muscles, make her limbs languid. The water bubbled and churned as if she was stirring it. Sweeping her worries away.

Janet closed her eyes, concentrating on Xander. She couldn't see the magic as she had before, but she could feel it, feel him. The mating bond, like all the magic in the realm, was a living thing.

She imagined it disappearing into her chest, like she'd witnessed when they'd bonded, and seen when Xander had healed her foot.

"My heart." She kept her voice low, but it still reverberated in the large cave, startling her. It shouldn't have, considering the same had happened when she'd called his name, but perhaps she'd been too distracted by the panic of being alone.

Don't be a coward.

Janet shook her head at herself and covered her left breast with her palm.

Over her heart.

Was the bond figurative or literal, disappearing into their bodies in that particular spot?

Xander had said their bond was already strengthening.

Were feelings — emotions — for each other the *result* or the *cause*?

She swallowed. The questions weren't any easier now than when they'd first come to her. Janet couldn't put words to how she felt for the Fae man she was supposed to spend the rest of her life with. She'd known him for half a year.

Janet had only been bonded to him for a day.

"It's too soon," she whispered.

First the bond, then running from her family as well as her Warrior.

Then…getting sucked here.

Overwhelming.

Nothing, not the magic, not her family, was taking what *she* wanted into consideration.

"What *do* I want?"

And what does Xander want?

He'd kissed her, she'd kissed him. She liked how it'd felt to be up against his chest, in his arms. Janet was definitely fond of the way he made her melt when his mouth moved over hers.

Xander had been so accepting of this whole thing. *From the start.*

Could he feel anything for her that wasn't some sort of magical obligation?

The ring on her left hand pulsed a dark purple. Janet stared. Confusion, desire, fears—about everything, Xander, her feelings, worry about getting home—it all stomped around her mind, making her shake in the warm water.

Knowing the ways of a man and a woman was one thing.

Experiencing it for the first time…was different than she'd imagined…or fantasized.

Intense.

But…better, right?

Nay. With magic involved, it was *worse*. Doubts thickened, threatening to overtake her.

Did either of them really have a choice?

It's too much.

Her head spun. Her chest ached; her heart was pounding so hard.

"Janet, what's wrong?"

His voice made her jump. It bounced around the large cavern, making it sound as if Xander had shouted.

Water sloshed against the sides of the pool, and he sought her, probably by sound alone.

When his beautiful eyes rested on her, Janet scorched to her toes, despite the water concealing her.

Her fated husband was too far away to see her nudity, but it didn't matter. Her neck, cheeks, even her ears burned.

"N-n-n-othin'," she called, averting her gaze as Xander approached. She wanted to cover herself, but her limbs refused to move. Besides, it wasn't like he'd be able to see her. Because of the natural eddies, the whirling water was hazy. So, even as he stood beside her, she was protected from his view.

Protected?

Xander was supposed to be her husband.

Should he not see her as naked as the day she was born?

He said nothing, but she *felt* him as if they were touching. If she reached out, Janet could brush her hand against his ankle, or his leg.

She still couldn't look at him.

"Are you well?"

Janet nodded. "Aye." She forced her face up. Met his gaze.

Color spread across Xander's high cheekbones. His powerful chest heaved as if he'd come in from a long run. Or a hard flight, as it were.

Desire pulsed across the mating bond, zinging to him and back. It crackled in the air, and awareness shot down Janet's spine. Her body tightened and melted at the same time, and it had little to do with the water.

She throbbed all over.

For him.

"Lass…" The word was a croak, and her insides trembled in response.

She sucked in a breath. "Join me."

Silence descended as her offer shocked them both.

Janet hadn't planned on saying the words aloud. She studied the surface of the flowing water. He was certainly going to think she was too forward now. Xander probably didn't want a *wanton* wife.

Embarrassment made her dizzy, threatened to swallow her whole. It was at odds with the passion in the air; palpable, heady, and holding her attention more than her inexperience or request.

The mating bond must be influencing her thoughts, her words.

Xander said nothing, but she heard the rustling of his linen tunic, the creak of his leather belt, even the scabbard of his sword thudding softly as he lowered it to the rocky floor.

Her heart threatened to exit her chest when he stepped into the water.

His wings reflected off the surface of the pool, but Janet kept her gaze down, despite the desire to look at his bare form. She'd seen his naked chest. Touched it. Been up against it. She wanted more.

Wanted all of Xander.

"Lass." His whisper was thick.

The mating bond was once again visible, glowing brightly beneath the surface of the water as he lowered himself next to her.

They reached for each other at the same time, but the kiss he placed on her lips was tender, gentle.

Not enough.

Xander pulled her into his arms.

They both shuddered from the full body contact.

Janet studied the iridescent wing in her line of sight, wanting to reach out, caress it. See if it was as smooth as it appeared, but she didn't have the courage. She closed her eyes against his shoulder, wiggling closer.

He caressed her neck, then her shoulder blades, making large circles down her back. His hand moved onto skin below the surface of the water. Xander groaned as he followed the curve of her bottom, but then he pulled away.

Janet lifted her head, meeting his violet eyes. "Why do ye stop?"

"Your brother demanded I return you home, virtue intact."

She frowned. "An' who is my brother ta decide such things fer me? 'Tis *my* body. *My* virtue." Janet didn't want to let irritation at Duncan ruin the energy between her and her fated husband, but it was already inching up from her gut.

How dare Duncan be a controlling barbarian?

"He cares about you."

Janet shook her head. "He's overbearin' like always."

Xander smirked but didn't comment.

"It might be Alex's place ta marry me off, but my laird dinnae be tha brother a' whom ye speak."

He threw his head back and laughed.

Janet stared at her winged Warrior.

Xander didn't laugh nearly enough. His handsome face was loose, radiant. Nowhere was the normal seriousness he wore like a shroud. His violet eyes twinkled, and he carried a lightness she'd never seen.

Happiness?

Her stomach flipped and she couldn't help the smile that curved her lips. Her irritation at her brother dissolved.

"You know your siblings well, my lady."

Janet paused. Should she chide him for formality or revel at his level of respect?

They were naked in a pool together, and she was in the circle of his embrace. An honorific was odd, considering their place—and role—to each other. "My lady?" she whispered.

Xander cocked his head to the side, studying her.

It was her turn to smirk. "We're…s'pposed ta be mates as ye say…married."

"Aye." He nodded and his pretty eyes were intense.

"So ye can discard the '*my lady*.'"

"Very well, lass."

She didn't like that any better. "Lass?" Her smirk slid into a grin. "Why dinnae ye say my name? Ye've only said it once—maybe twice—since we've arrived."

"Janet." Her name rolled off Xander's tongue and she trembled against him.

Janet reached for him, resting her hand against his cheek. His skin was smooth, only the barest stubble grazing her palm. Fae did not have hair anywhere but on their heads, but Fae men could grow beards. Maybe it just took longer than most humans.

Desire surged through their bond—from both of them.

Xander's gaze locked onto her face, and his lips parted.

She wanted him to kiss her, but he didn't.

Janet let her hand drop into the water and broke their eye contact. "I-I-I'm sorry."

"'Tis fine." He lifted her palm and traced his jaw with her fingertips, making his skin sheen with water droplets. Then Xander turned her hand over and kissed her knuckles. "You can touch me anywhere you'd like."

She nodded because she hadn't a clue what to say to that. Janet wanted to burrow into him, kiss him, touch him as he'd just offered.

She wanted to give herself to him.

Xander gently cupped her face. "We belong to each other, Janey."

"Janey?" She smiled. "Duncan an' Alex called me

tha' as a lass."

"I know," he whispered.

Janet stared into his violet eyes. They were darker than normal, and her heart stuttered.

She tilted her face up and Xander dipped his head down. She met his mouth with hers, opening for him immediately.

He tugged her against him; she slipped her arms around his neck and kissed him harder as his tongue danced with hers.

Xander's erection pressed against Janet's thigh, but it didn't shock or scare her. She burned for him, pulsing between her legs.

He caressed the sides of her breasts, and she leaned away as he spread kisses down her neck.

She let her head fall back to allow him access, and he dragged his tongue along the edge of her jaw.

Janet cried out when his fingertips brushed her nipples. Then his large, calloused hands were there, cupping and kneading her, making the already taut, oversensitive skin ache.

Xander continued downward, dragging his hand across her belly beneath the water.

Her muscles jumped as he went, quivering in anticipation of more. She breathed his name when he touched her center.

No one had ever put their fingers there, save herself during a bath.

Pleasure shot all over her body when he rubbed

the tight bundle of nerves at the top of her sex.

Janet gasped and made a grab for his wrist. "Wh-wha' are ye doin'?"

Xander kissed her in answer, nibbling her bottom lip. "Let me touch you, Janey. Let me love you." He moved his fingers as he spoke, scattering her thoughts.

She couldn't have told him no even if she'd wanted to. Which she *most certainly* did not.

"Dinnae stop," she breathed.

He traced the seam of her lips with his tongue, but it wasn't enough.

Janet fused their mouths, swallowing a groan from Xander.

Deepening their kiss, he moved his hand in rhythm with his tongue, rocking his hips beneath hers.

She reclined into the side of the pool as Xander pressed closer, his chest hovering over her breasts, his nipples brushing hers. His arousal burned her hip, but he made no attempt to push inside her. He just kissed her again, teasing her core with clever fingers.

The water swirled around them, the steam making her already clouded mind even hazier.

Something was happening. An odd pressure was building that she didn't understand. It didn't hurt; it felt *good*, but it wasn't enough.

Her sex ached, felt empty, despite the attention her Fae Warrior was paying to it.

He probed her entrance but didn't plunge his finger inside.

She wanted to beg him but hadn't the strength to speak.

Her hips rocked of their own accord and Xander kept kissing her as he rubbed her beneath the water. Janet writhed against him, moaning. Whimpering. Making sounds she'd never uttered in her life.

He nipped her earlobe and a tremor shot down her spine. "Let go, lass."

She wanted to ask him what he meant, but his statement was a trigger. Her body knew the answer. Something snapped inside her.

Janet threw her head back as her muscles contracted and released on their own. She had no control. Pleasure made her scream his name, and she clutched at Xander's powerful shoulders.

The pool was spinning, like her head, her thoughts.

She crushed her eyes shut as Xander's mouth descended to take hers again, but she was boneless and kissing him back took concentration she couldn't muster.

He gathered her close, resting his forehead against hers. They were melded against the pool and each other, chest to breasts, panting in time.

"Goddess, lass. You're beautiful, Janey."

She should have been embarrassed, but she wasn't. "Xander…"

Her fated husband smiled, and it was as gorgeous as he was. "Thank you for letting me show you pleasure."

Janet wanted more, so much more, but she couldn't find her voice to confess it.

"Let's dry off and sleep," Xander whispered, kissing her tenderly. His erection still seared her hip, as hard as the rocks beneath them and just as smooth.

She wanted to touch it, touch him. Janet had never… "What abou' ye?"

"Not tonight, Janey. I won't take you tonight."

Janet swallowed, once again losing her courage to disagree.

Does he not want me?

Or is he respecting my brother?

One answer hurt, the other irritated.

Xander caressed her cheek. His gaze was as soft as the touch; it pleased and caused pain at the same time.

Janet's chest burned. Tears stung her eyes and she refused to give in. She gently disengaged from him and couldn't look at him as she exited the pool, wrapping herself in the blanket.

He said nothing as he dried and dressed, but her stomach dropped when he donned his trews, then his boots.

"Ye dinnae be sleepin' with me?" Janet tried not to choke on her words. Forced her eyes onto his so she couldn't accuse herself of being a coward.

The mating bond pulsed. She could see it easier than before; it glowed an even brighter gold.

She couldn't sense his feelings, like he'd said

they'd be able to eventually, but her own mind was full of chaos. She couldn't order her thoughts. Her limbs were warm and sated, but her heart heavy.

Xander squared his broad shoulders. He was still aroused, but she tore her eyes away from that part of him. "I need to go outside and make sure we're still safe. Then I'll join you."

Janet said nothing as she watched him exit the cavern.

Called herself a fool for feeling close to him, but she couldn't regret letting him touch her.

That had been perfect.

She swiped at the first tear that coursed down her cheek, but ignored the ones that followed it.

chapter twelve

is head reeled, pulse thundering in his temples, in time with the pounding in his cock. Xander buried his hand in his short hair.

She'd been so sweet.

Why did you walk away?

He'd wanted nothing more than to take what she'd offered…take *her.*

Despite Xander initiating the contact, Janet *had* offered herself to him. Even without words, her body had spoken volumes.

He could've had her.

Could be having her right now.

Hadn't he been worried about the consequences of the mating bond? Getting sick if they didn't consummate?

Janet had been spread before him. Rubbing her body into his, kissing him back with fervor that belied her innocence.

His mind spun—then and now. Xander had been swept away.

In her.

Unmanly shivers crept over his unsated body, and he started to shake. His wings twitched, so he flexed, then extended them. Xander wanted to take off. Fly away. High above the Falls, feel the wind in his ears and flowing over his body as he sliced through the sky. He could soar on a thermal, close his eyes, and gather his thoughts.

Make a plan.

Which he needed to, especially since questioning Mikhias had gotten him nowhere.

Looking up at the full moon, Xander flapped his wings again. Moving air swirled around his face.

"Nay." His voice startled him, and he locked his jaw.

Janet.

Xander couldn't leave her again, no matter the chaos in his mind. Besides, he didn't know what his father and the Fae Warriors were up to. Mikhias hadn't known.

Had they discovered where he and Janet were?

He doubted it.

They would've stormed the Falls if they had, wouldn't they?

Xander and Alana might have discovered the cavern and the hot springs, but it wasn't that difficult to find.

Should he and Janet move on?

There wasn't another place to go, really.

Safety was an illusion no matter *where* they chose to hide.

Mikhias and Ruark had angered his father and the

king when Xander had escaped with his wife. He'd compelled Mikhias to tell him what Ruark knew, as well. They weren't privy to any pertinent information. Not the guard schedule, not why his captain father had called the battalion away from the Stones.

Both warriors had lost ranking when they'd lost him.

"Bollocks."

Xander had cleared Mikhias's mind after he'd questioned him, ordering the Warrior to forget their encounter, but he couldn't do the same for the unconscious Ruark. He'd said a disorientation spell over Ruark's still form, but there was no guarantee it would work. Either spell could be reversed by a mage. If their minds were probed, Xander would be discovered anyway.

When he'd returned to the cavern, he'd intended on sharing an abbreviated version of what had happened with Janet.

He hadn't planned on what'd happened between them, but Xander wouldn't have changed anything.

Well, except for his loss of control.

Even if—when—they consummated their bond, he needed to keep a clear head. Despite how much he burned for Janet.

He'd promised he'd get her home.

Xander would.

Using all the magic he could muster.

The Human Realm.

He'd live there. With Janet. At the MacLeod stronghold. At the expense of a piece of himself.

Again.

Tremors racked his frame.

Xander sucked in a breath and pumped his wings. He spread his arms and tilted his head, diving off the ledge.

His body plummeted, then he spread his wings and righted himself, flying close enough to the river to skim his fingers over the water. Unlike the pool, the water here was frigid, shocking his limb all the way to his elbow.

Perhaps he should plunge into it. The cold might cool his ardor, sweep his mind clean.

Cursing, Xander whipped upward, flying toward the moon. He passed the entrance to the cave, muttering his invisibility spell. He tried to avoid looking at the Falls.

Flashes of Janet in his arms, naked against his skin danced into his mind. She was supple, soft, and fit his form as if she'd been made for him.

She was *made for me.*

After all, that was why they were fated, was it not?

Xander sighed, closing his eyes as he soared higher.

He wanted her.

Nay.

Needed her.

He also needed all the advantage he could muster

to get them home. Consummating their mating bond made sense. Neither of them could afford the sickness of denial, and Xander didn't know how much time they had.

Janet wanted him, too. That was plain.

Even if he went back to the Stones and stunned—or killed—whatever guards were there, it would take him precious time to open the portal. What Alana could do in several minutes had always been harder for Xander since his cousin had more magic.

Concentrating, gathering the magic around him, and focusing on the Faery Stones would take time and most of his energy. He couldn't risk Janet's life unless he was sure they would get to the Realm of the Humans on the *first* attempt.

Opening the portal would *have* to be a certainty.

Then again, joining with his fated mate might increase his magic, even though she was a human with none.

Xander should march back into the cavern, slip into bed with her and make her his.

Balance was the key.

Right?

Something he'd never struggled with in his long life.

Alana had many times accused him of being too logical, never thinking with his heart. His cousin was driven by hers. He'd always blamed it on her empathic magic as well as her gender, but perhaps *she* had the way of it.

His cousin was no stranger to taking a leap of faith.

Xander had never closed his eyes and jumped without looking. He strategized. Thought things out before acting. He was a soldier. It was in his blood.

He'd seen the tears in Janet's sapphire eyes when he'd muttered his excuse. Felt her hurt and disappointment through their infant bond. Xander had wanted to whip around, rip his clothes back off and join her on the mattress he'd secured for her comfort.

Apologize and wipe that look off her face. Worship her body.

Instead, he'd sucked in a breath and put some distance between them. Because *he'd* needed it.

Selfish brute.

His reluctant mate wasn't so *reluctant* anymore. At least she hadn't been in the pool.

Xander should be rejoicing that Janet was no longer rejecting him. Their encounter in the small hot spring was the first of that kind for her.

He botched how it'd ended. Xander should've reassured her. Told her how perfect it'd been. How much he wanted more — wanted her. He'd burned for her from that first kiss on the beach, and now that ache was worse.

Fate had been kind to him in that regard; no doubt he'd always desire Janet in his bed.

Xander flipped in the air. Flew upside down so the blood rushed to his head until his temples pounded.

His cock was still aching. Still half-hard, but there was no relief in sight. He'd no desire to bury his hand in his trews and take care of matters. Release would have no real meaning until it was inside his wife.

A shudder racked Xander's frame at the images in his head with that thought.

How long could he resist her?

He had no real desire to do so.

Taking her was *right*; driven by fate.

Xander was going to have to reach for balance in any way he could. For the first time in his adult life, his vows were to a woman that *wasn't* his cousin.

He couldn't fail Janet MacLeod.

chapter thirteen

"You. Will. Not." Xander lowered his voice and spit the words.

His blood boiled. It wasn't often he lost his temper, but his lass was firing him in more than one way.

As Janet had over the past three days, so many times he'd lost count.

He'd been waiting on edge to see which one of them would snap first. Being cooped up had stressed her, he'd felt it in their bond as well as seen it. She'd taken to pacing in their hiding place.

Janet's sapphire eyes flashed; he didn't need the artificial light in the wide cavern to see her ire. "Ye have nay tha right ta tell me what ta do."

Through their mating bond, he felt her anger, but his own rebounded back. No doubt she could feel it. Xander still couldn't read her mind, but her feelings were becoming more and more transparent the longer they were together.

Especially sleeping side by side on the mattress he'd magically stolen. The past three nights, he'd only joined her because he hadn't been able to endure watching her sleep and not be with her. He'd crawled under the soft blankets, trying to blame it on the bond tugging at him, but it was more than that.

Janet's sleep-warmed body had turned toward him as if by instinct, but Xander had restrained himself from reaching for her. Holding her. He'd not even kissed her since the first night—the night she'd shattered in his arms in the heated pool.

Awkwardness had settled over them. Touching, even by accident, had slipped into *uncomfortable,* although they both craved it.

Since he'd pulled back, being trapped with Janet at Grànnda Falls had only served to make him yearn for her. Flying at night had done nothing to clear his head. Even jumping into the frigid river had failed to cool his ardor. Afterward, he'd been more agitated than before.

Xander felt her hurt every time she met his eyes. Janet thought he was rejecting her when he was just trying to keep them both safe. He'd masked his own thoughts and feelings as best he could and hadn't explained how wrong she was.

He didn't merely *want* her.

Xander burned for her.

He was torn between desire and the drive to get her home safely. Yet, in the back of his mind, he worried if they didn't consummate their union, magic from the bond would start to affect them.

Xander would get weak, sick.

Since Janet's Fae blood was minute, it could go either way for her. She could become the more ill of the two, or perhaps the magic wouldn't have something to latch on and drain, so she wouldn't get sick at all.

He teetered back and forth between what he wanted and what he'd vowed.

For her.

To protect her.

Xander *couldn't* lose control.

"I've every right. As your mate. Your husband."

Janet's jaw flexed and she narrowed her eyes. "We've no' wed."

"Perhaps in the Human Realm, but we're bonded, as you well know. You're my mate—my wife. You're mine."

Her breasts heaved and he tried not to stare. Color spread across her high cheekbones and her glare alone could have flayed him open, had it the power. The mating bond pulsed red. So did her ring, as it too sensed her emotions.

"Dinnae tell me what ta do." Janet threw her dark hair over one shoulder and made a move to slide past him, on her way out of the cave as she'd threatened.

Xander had made the mistake of taking her out to the ledge the night before, so Janet knew she didn't have to get doused by the falls to leave the cavern. However, she'd get hurt if she tried to scale the face of the cliffside.

He moved fast.

Xander hopped into the air, pumping his wings once, then twice more. His muscles and magic alike burned—maybe now from *overuse* since he'd been back in the realm of his birth. He snaked an arm around Janet's waist and lifted her from the rocky cave floor.

She yelped, then struggled against his hold.

He ignored her, holding firmly but trying not to crush her. After gliding to the back of the massive cavern, he landed a foot or so from the wall.

Xander pressed his mate into the smoothest part of the natural surface and blocked her in. He put his palms to the stone on either side of Janet.

Their bodies were close, but no longer touching, and he had to stop himself from leaning into her lush breasts. Flashes of her bare in his arms shot through his mind. Her scent tickled his nose and made his cock twitch. He tried to tamp down his ardor.

The globes he'd summoned to brighten their shelter made her beautiful face radiant.

Janet didn't shirk away when their gazes collided. Anger skittered across her expression, sparked in those deep blue eyes. Reverberated in their bond, too.

His admiration of her rose even higher. Xander's MacLeod lass was strong. That he'd already known. However, he was tall and broad, intentionally intimidating her.

She wasn't afraid of him, even trapped against a cave wall with no space between their bodies.

By the Goddess, she's gorgeous.

"Jus' because we're—"

"As difficult as it may be, I need you to mind me."

Janet scowled. "*Mind* ye?"

"If we do not stick together, we're not going to get back to the Human Realm. Capture by Fae Warriors means death. I'm a banished traitor. You're human. We've gone over this many times now, Janey."

Fear Xander hadn't seen in three days flickered in her eyes and she nodded. Her full mouth parted, and it took all he was made of not to kiss her. Claim her like he'd wanted to in the pool, like he'd been resisting since that night.

His promise to Alana that he wouldn't fight the mating bond burst into his mind, but he ignored it.

That's not what this is about.

Right?

He cleared his throat. "I'm sorry I grabbed you. But you cannot leave this cave. King Fillan knows we're here. Worse, he knows *I* am here. I can't risk taking you back to the Faery Stones just yet."

"When then?"

"I don't know." Xander had told her of his talk with Mikhias and what was involved with opening the Stones. She'd said she wanted to help. Janet didn't like feeling helpless. Magic, as well as knowledge from getting to know her over the past few days told him that.

"I still trust ye..." Her whisper was painful, despite her words.

"Good."

Silence fell, but Xander didn't move away from

her. He couldn't.

They stared at each other.

Janet swallowed and he wanted to kiss her throat. "Wha' happened?"

Her question was so low, had Xander not been so close, he would've missed it.

He frowned. "What do you mean?"

"Ye…an'…me?" Hurt skipped across her face, as well as pulsed in the bond. "The other nigh'…"

"This was forced upon us." Xander gentled his voice.

"I…thought tha' stopped matterin'. At least, it did fer me." Janet closed her eyes.

The vulnerability he saw when their gazes met again made his heart jump. Xander felt her nerves through the mating bond.

She was reaching out to him.

For him.

The rest would be up to Xander.

He wished he could read her mind at that moment more than any before. Xander had always thought she was beautiful. Had always watched her — even before the ring had revealed they were mates. He'd been intrigued with Janet MacLeod since he'd learned he couldn't read her mind. Never would he have figured it was because she was supposed to be his.

Supposed to be mine.

She is *mine.*

Mine.

"I hurt you," he croaked.

Janet nodded and lowered her lashes.

Her honesty was refreshing. It touched him, made him hurt *for* her.

"I'm sorry," Xander whispered.

She didn't respond. Wouldn't look at him.

He caressed her cheek and cupped her face, tugging up so she had to meet his eyes. The tears in hers rocked him. Xander couldn't muster any words. He had to wipe that look away.

Now.

Xander dipped his head down and covered her mouth with his.

Janet moved into his kiss, not away, snaking her arms around his neck. She arched her body, rubbing him from chest to waist.

His cock hardened to the point of pain, straining against his breeches.

She opened for him without urging. Their tongues mingled, danced, and dueled.

He kissed her harder, slanting his mouth over hers again and again.

Janet was right with him, her fervor belying her lack of experience, just like in the pool. She clung to him, molding her body to his.

By the Goddess, he wanted her. Three days had been too long.

Xander tore his mouth away, panting hard against her breasts. "I want you," he breathed. If he kissed her much longer, he was liable to lift her skirts and plunge into her body.

It wasn't fair to her.

Janet had never given herself to a man.

It fired his blood to know he would be her one and only — *ever* — but Xander needed to temper his lust and take her properly.

Gently, the first time.

Her breathing was rough too, and his erection jolted when her pink tongue shot out to moisten her kiss-swollen bottom lip. Janet's dark hair was disheveled, and her face flushed. Passion and need throbbed from her to him through their mating bond.

Xander bit back a groan.

Awareness and desire shone in that sapphire gaze. "I…burn, Xander."

The confession made his blood sing. He flexed his wings as a tremor shot down his spine. His arousal pulsed and kicked. Threatened to blow as it rubbed against the soft fabric of his trews. "You want me, lass, like I want you. I feel it."

"I'm hot all over. Worse than t'other nigh'. I…feel as if my body dinnae be my own. I…need ta touch ye. Ye ta touch me again. Is this magic?"

Her words lit him up from the inside out, as good as a caress trailing his whole body, intensified through the golden rope between them.

Xander managed a laugh. "I'd like to think *that* 'tis me, as an accomplished lover, but the drive you feel is partly because of our bond, aye."

Janet's cheeks went crimson, but she didn't avert her eyes. "Alana said if we dinnae—" she swallowed, "make love, we get sick." The last part was so low he'd almost missed it.

He leaned in, his mouth hovering over hers. "Do not doubt that I want you. It has little to do with magic."

Those blue eyes went wide but then slipped shut as she met his lips for another kiss. "Now?" Janet breathed into his mouth.

Xander gathered her to him, moving them away from the side of the cavern. He couldn't resist her or their bond any longer. Didn't want to. "Now, my Janey," he whispered.

She paused, looking up at him, a smile playing at her kiss-swollen lips. "I want ta be *yer* Janey." The declaration made her flushed face even redder, and his stomach somersaulted.

Xander kissed her cheeks, then pressed his lips to her forehead. "As you wish."

Janet took an audible breath. "What do *ye* wish, Xander?"

"I belong to you. I told you such in the pool." He dipped low to kiss her throat.

"Fate. Nay considerin' what ye an' I want. A part a' me…needs ta ken it, Xander. Ye said ye want me…but what a' us? The mating bond. The o'her night in the pool, ye said ye dinnae take me. Was that fer my brother's benefit?"

"I made a vow to Alana I wouldn't fight this."

Janet's expression fell and she averted her eyes.

Hurt thumped through the magic that joined them, and Xander regretted his choice of words. "Lass," he whispered.

She still wouldn't look at him.

"What I mean to say is I don't *want* to fight the mating bond."

Only then did she meet his gaze, her sapphire eyes misty. "Truly?"

"Truly."

chapter fourteen

Janet threw her arms around his neck and fused her mouth to his.

Xander didn't fight the press of her body or her kiss. He twined his tongue around hers, exploring her, feasting on her.

He tore at the bodice covering her ivory leine. The ties weren't cooperating with his trembling fingers. He needed her naked, *now*. Xander wished she was still clad in only her chemise, like when they'd shed their wet clothing, like every night when he'd lain beside her.

It'd been torture watching the rise and fall of her breasts as she slept. Resisting the urge — the drive from the bond — to touch her, like he'd done in the pool.

Cover Janet's body with his.

Take her. Make her his.

"No more." Xander pressed the words into her mouth.

Janet pulled back, confusion dancing across her pretty visage. "No more?"

He laughed and kissed her, hard and fast. "I'm sorry, *mò aingeal*. I was speaking to myself."

She smiled, slow and sensual. "Angel?"

"Aye."

"But yer tha one with wings." Janet cocked her head to one side. "Yer Gaelic is good."

"Most Gaelic is not so different from Fae. We don't use the word *angel*, but I know of it; I know what it means." Xander tightened his grip on his mate. He pumped his wings, lifting them into the air.

She wrapped herself around him as he glided the short distance to the mattress.

"I'll do this right. Make it special for you," he whispered when they'd landed.

Janet stared up at him, trust and desire shining from those blue eyes. Pink graced her high cheekbones, from their kisses as well as a sudden shyness that made Xander smile.

His wife nodded. "I want ta be with ye," she said finally. "Tha rest dinnae matter."

Through the mating bond he felt her sincerity. Xander caressed her cheeks, unable to keep his hands to himself. This time, he didn't have to. "Undress, *mò aingeal*. I want to see you, like I didn't get to the other night. The water hid you from me."

Janet stepped back, finishing the job he'd been unable to do with her bodice. The stiff material fell away from her body, her leine loosening, hiding her slender waist and the curve of her hips, the fullness of her breasts.

Does not matter.

He'd see her in moments.

Xander stood transfixed as her skirts fell, pooling at her feet on the cavern floor.

Janet pulled her leine up and off, and it joined the navy-blue wool.

He could see through her chemise, the skin of her nipples darker than the rest, teasing him. His cock pulsed and he reached for the ties on his trews, but his fingers blundered. Xander couldn't stop watching his wife, and she wasn't even nude yet.

"Xander?" She paused, her hands bunching fabric at her waist.

"Aye, *mò aingeal*?"

"Yer…yer…"

"I will disrobe. Your beauty stuns me, lass." Xander swallowed because his mouth had gone dry as the truth drifted from his lips.

Her face went even redder, but his lass didn't look away. She lifted the chemise over her head without loosening the ties at the neckline. Janet dropped it to the rocky floor, her perfect breasts heaving as if she'd taken a breath.

Xander lost the ability to catch his own. Through the blessed — *blessed* — magic globes in the large space, he could see every inch of his fated mate.

Gorgeous was too weak a word. Ethereal *perfection* was before him.

Light surrounded her like an aura. The mating bond shone brightly, as if their link had strengthened even more.

His eyes trailed her frame, trying to take her all in at once. He'd felt her curves in the pool, but now Xander could see them. Her slender waist, her rounded hips, her long, long legs. His gaze rested at the apex of her thighs.

Tight dark curls guarded her core. That should've given him pause, since he'd never had a human lover, and Fae women were bare over their sexes, but it did nothing to detract from Janet's allure. His drive, his desire was to possess her.

Now.

"*Mò aingeal*," Xander croaked, but he didn't care. "Come here, lass. Come to me, *mò aingeal*."

Janet didn't hesitate as she closed the distance between them.

Tremors started all over his whole body, including jarring his wings as he reached for her.

She wrapped her arms around him, the heat of her body seeping through his tunic. He dragged his hands down her bare back, palming her smooth skin. Following the curve of her bottom made Xander groan, and his wife shudder in his arms.

"Xander," she whispered. "Please. I need ta touch yer skin."

Forcing himself to release her, Xander whipped off his tunic. He didn't push Janet away from the ties on his trews, letting her loosen the garment. His cock kicked, begging the same kind of attention.

She helped him push the breeches off his hips.

Janet's eyes stayed below his waist, even after the brushed leather hit the cave floor.

His cock liked the appraisal, springing forward.

Janet reached for him, but then paused. She met his eyes and embarrassment rippled through their bond.

Xander screamed at himself to relax. "You…can touch me…anywhere. As I told you…" He shoved the thick words out of his mouth.

She nodded, stroking his length, her fingers skimming his most sensitive skin.

He gasped, and his hips pitched forward of their own accord.

"No hair," Janet whispered. She encircled him, exploring with a bravery he admired, but shot his excitement beyond his limit. Her hand continued down, cupping him from below.

"What do you know of such things, my innocent lass?" Xander's voice was too fragmented for his tease to carry, but his wife must've caught it, because amusement darted across her pretty face.

"*Innocent* dinnae mean naïve, my husband."

The words zinged like a caress down his spine as she continued to move her hand.

Xander was about to come out of his skin. He stood trembling in her grip until he could take no more. His bollocks tightened; his erection kicked as if he would orgasm. He needed her to stop before he released all over her hands, but words would not form. He groaned.

Janet's eyes sought his face. "Did I…hurt ye?"

He grabbed her knuckles and lavished kisses all over them. "No, lass. Your touch is…perfect. But…you make me burn for you. If you continue, this'll be over before it starts."

"Oh." She looked down.

Xander reached for her, making her meet his gaze, tucking a strand of her dark hair behind one ear. "This is a good thing, lass. I want you." He brushed his lips over hers, and Janet moved into his body, pressing her lush breasts against him.

They both gasped at the contact.

"Have me, make me yers."

"Oh, *mò aingeal*, you are already mine." He kissed her again, and Janet kissed him back hard, rubbing her tongue into his.

His body was on fire as Xander pushed her into the stolen bedding. His chest brushed her nipples as he followed her down, settling into the cradle of her body.

Janet moaned, gripping the back of his neck. Then her hands were on his shoulders, going down as far as she could reach. She caressed the base of his wings and Xander shook. He closed his eyes and dragged warm wet kisses along her exposed throat.

"Xander." His name was a breathless whisper that flipped his heart; his erection pulsed in response.

He dragged his tongue down her collarbone and nibbled the hard tips of her nipples.

Janet arched into him. "Please…"

Xander teased his fingers down her belly, and she squirmed. He caressed her inner thighs, then finally buried his hand in the heaven between her legs. "Wet. *Mò aingeal,* you're already wet for me." A shudder racked his frame. He rubbed the bundle of nerves at the top of her sex.

Little whimpers fell from her lips and when she clutched him close, scrambling for another kiss, Xander couldn't take it anymore.

She was ready, and he had to have her.

"Lass, I need you."

"Aye," Janet said. "I dinnae endure anamore!"

Xander slipped a hand between them, positioning his arousal at her sex. The drive to make them one took over, and he didn't pause to consider her innocence.

He filled her to the hilt with one stroke forward.

They both gasped.

The mating bond went radiant.

Xander squinted against the brightness, warmth crashing over his whole body. His wings shook and shifted, and heat settled in his chest, so hot it should've scorched, but it didn't.

Rightness enveloped him, like it had on the beach when he'd first kissed Janet.

Emotion smacked into him, and he dipped his head, taking her mouth and starting to thrust, because he couldn't do anything else.

She whimpered but moved her lips under his.

Xander pulled away, opening his eyes as the fog started to fade, and his heart jumped. He'd joined them roughly. Janet had been a virgin. "Goddess, *mò aingeal*. Are you well? Did I hurt you?"

Her sapphire eyes were hazy and heavy-lidded. "It dinnae hurt anymore. I…burn…fer ye ta move within me."

"As you wish," he groaned and slanted his mouth over hers again, shifting his hips slowly, rocking until he found a gentle rhythm.

Janet broke their kiss and threw her head back. "More."

Through their bond, he *felt* her word, her demand, as well as her pleasure. He swallowed a moan as the sensations washed over him like a physical caress.

Xander felt her *completely*.

He couldn't read her mind, but he could feel her emotions. They mixed with his, threatening to overwhelm as his body demanded he take her hard, make her feel him from the inside out.

Janet tilted her hips and rubbed her breasts into his chest, as if she could read *his* mind.

He shivered but couldn't refuse her. Xander pulled back and plunged forward. His wife met his thrust, moaning her encouragement as well as squeezing his rear end with both hands.

Raw feelings, every emotion from Janet melded into his chest, guiding his hips like a command. His were the same, falling into the bond until magic was all he could sense; it surrounded them like a bubble.

Xander couldn't look away from Janet's sapphire eyes, either.

Their touches, kisses, thrusts had no rhythm. He couldn't think. Xander could only *feel*.

Janet maintained his gaze as her body stiffened beneath his, and she called his name. Her nails dug into his shoulders, and she arched into his chest. Her orgasm pitched him over the edge.

His ears roared, but Xander couldn't tell if it was Grànnda Falls or magic-enhanced-pleasure so sharp his head spun. He panted her name like a mantra.

Her core contracted, milking him. His cock kicked and he spilled himself inside her.

They both shook from head to toe, and he struggled for breath. His wings vibrated.

Never...*ever*...in all his years had Xander experienced something like taking Janet.

She still clutched his shoulders, but he didn't care if she drew blood. His head spun.

The bond dominated his vision, but instead of appearing like the rope they'd both been used to seeing, they were surrounded in golden light, like two melded auras where their bodies were touching.

"Xander?"

Words wouldn't form, so he lowered his mouth and took hers, pushing his tongue deep.

Janet kissed him back, and it melted into something heated and languorous, leaving them both moaning and squeezing each other tight.

"*Mò aingeal*," he finally managed, the words tangled in the movement of their lips.

"Xander," she repeated.

Xander shifted his hips, his softening arousal slipping from her body. He rolled to his side, taking her with him.

"Hold me?" She snuggled into his chest, throwing her arm across his middle.

"Aye, *mò aingeal*, always."

Janet flashed a smile that had his stomach flipping.

After about ten minutes of companionable silence and sweet kisses, he talked her into letting him get something to clean them up. His head spun as he wiped the blood from his sex and thighs.

She was no longer innocent.

Janet was wholly his.

Xander's head and heart were floating, wrapped up in the golden magic of the mating bond...and in her.

He gently cleaned his mate with a scrap of linen saturated with warm water from the pool, smiling at her pink cheeks.

Xander scrambled to clear his mind, but all he could see was the lass waiting for him, opening her arms to pull him into a warm embrace.

By the Goddess, I still have to protect her.

Get her home.

He vowed to maintain the control to keep his angel safe.

No matter what he had to do.

chapter fifteen

She stilled against Xander. He'd pulled her back to him as soon as he'd returned to the bed, but something wasn't right. Her fated husband was stiff, even though he'd plastered Janet to his broad chest. "What's wrong?"

"Nothing, lass." He punctuated his words by pressing his lips to her temple.

Nay.

"I…feel…wha' ye do. Yer….unsure." Hurt surged up from Janet's gut and she shook, even though his warmth surrounded her.

Her Warrior wasn't being honest.

It was worse than the rejection she'd felt after he'd touched her in the pool.

Now Janet *belonged* to Xander.

"Do…do…ye regret bein' with me?" she whispered.

"Nay." His voice was hard.

Air rushed from her lungs as she felt Xander's truth from their bond.

"Look at me, *mò aingeal.*"

She didn't refuse the order. Janet locked gazes with his beautiful violet eyes.

"*You* are perfect. I regret nothing." Xander cupped her cheeks.

Again, truth reverberated from the link they shared.

Janet relaxed against him, reveling in his heat. She felt protected, but something bothered her. Despite being able to sense him in a way she'd never thought possible of another, there was *something* missing.

What is he not telling me?

She was new to magic, after all. Xander had been using it his whole life.

What if she only felt what he *wanted* her to?

She stared into his face but saw—felt—nothing to worry about.

He looked back upon her with tenderness and warmth. When Xander reached out and stroked her face, she leaned into him, sighing.

"Can we have a wedding?" Janet blurted. Heat crept up her neck, settling in her cheeks. She chided herself for the embarrassment. After what they'd shared, it was silly.

A smile bloomed on his delectable lips, and her stomach flipped.

"Aye, if you wish it."

She nodded, then regained some composure. She smirked. "Come ta think on it, my brothers dinnae allow otherwise—neither of 'em."

Xander chuckled and her insides tingled.

Seeing him relaxed—as well as *feeling* it—was

detrimental to her ability to think properly. He was even more beautiful.

The golden rope of the bond was visible when she touched him, but he was also surrounded by radiant light.

Janet raised her hand, fingers spread wide, also glowing. "Light, everywhere," she whispered. "What is this?"

"Our bond, *mò aingeal.*"

Her stomach fluttered and she nestled even closer.

Xander rubbed her back with long, soft strokes. Her limbs melted, going even more boneless.

She slipped her arms around his neck, kissing his jaw line and flattening her breasts against his chest.

He made a noise in his throat and squeezed his arms around her.

Janet reached for his wings.

Xander shivered, so she dragged her fingertips over the iridescent flesh.

"Can ye feel tha'?" she whispered.

"Aye."

She pulled back to meet his eyes.

He nodded. "They're a part of my body. Like any other skin. They can be injured and cause pain. They bleed when torn."

Frowning, Janet continued to caress him. The flesh felt like any other, except it shimmered like a prism, different colors popping up when they caught the light of the magic globes. "But ye dinnae have them in the

Human Realm."

"My wings are a part of my magic, which is diminished in the Human Realm."

"So, ye dinnae be able ta fly."

"Not there, nay."

"But..." Janet lowered her lashes. Sadness sat heavily in her stomach. She clenched her jaw to keep tears at bay. The strength of the emotion washed over her, confusing, but she hurt *for* him.

How hard missing a piece of himself must be...

Xander shifted. "But what, *mò aingeal*?"

She looked down, grateful her dark hair curtained her face, but her husband tucked some strands behind her ear.

He pulled her closer and wrapped his arms around her, enclosing them both with his wings at the same time.

Janet smiled, but she had to swallow, too.

"What has you upset?"

"When we're home—*my* home—in tha Human Realm, a part of ye is missin'." She shuddered—and felt worse.

"Our home."

"Our home?" Her heart missed a beat when she felt sincerity through the bond.

"Aye. The Human Realm is my home now. I don't regret it. I belong at Alana's side. I'm sworn to protect her. Angus, too, since he's her lad. And the bairn she carries. They're my responsibility, as well."

Something akin to jealousy hit in a wave. Janet tried not to show it in her face when she met his gaze. "She's, yer cousin."

"Aye. More than that, she's family. *They* are family. Alana is more like a sister to me than cousin."

What am I to you?

Janet bit back the question.

Wife.

Now lover.

Xander had said he wouldn't fight the bond—that he didn't want to. Was it still a vow to Alana, or for her, as his fated mate?

Janet tried to ignore the hurt that made her chest ache. He would feel it. She swallowed a wince. "Ye sacrificed fer her." Her voice had an odd edge, even to her own ears. She couldn't look at him. "Ye love her."

Not me.

She chided herself for foolishness. They'd been bonded without wishing it—and for mere days. Made love so they wouldn't get sick.

What else did she expect?

It was all so new.

I don't love him, either. But…could I?

"Aye," Xander said. It was as if he was answering her question, like he'd read her mind.

Janet jumped, reminding herself that he was only affirming that he loved his cousin, not her.

"I need to thank Alana, *mò aingeal.*"

When Janet finally was able to look at him, her

fated mate was smiling.

"Because of my cousin's desire to be with your brother, I found you, my Janey."

She swallowed again and her lips parted.

Xander tugged her closer, burying his hand in the hair at the back of her neck. He pressed his mouth to hers.

Janet didn't fight him. She opened, inviting his tongue inside, like she'd welcomed him into her body. Her sex throbbed. She wanted him again.

Despite the pain of first penetration, making love with Xander had given her more pleasure than she'd ever imagined the intimacies of a man and woman would—or could.

She dragged her hand down his muscled chest and kissed him harder.

Xander responded by slanting his mouth over hers again, groaning as their tongues mingled, then dueled. His erection burned her thigh, and her core pulsed.

Janet felt empty.

Only the man kissing her to oblivion could fill her.

Hooking her leg over his hip made him grunt, but he didn't fight when she tugged him on top of her.

He chuckled into their kiss. "In a rush, *mò aingeal*?"

"I need ye." Janet panted as the golden magic made her head spin as much as his mouth moving over hers. "I…feel *everythin'*," she whispered.

"It's the magic. It's everywhere, but it flows *through* us, too." Xander cupped her breasts, teasing her nipples with his thumbs.

"'Twill be like this always?" She had to force the words out, because his ministrations scattered her thoughts and shot heat to her center.

"I don't know how strong it'll be once we're no longer in this realm." He dragged wet kisses down her neck. He rocked his hips, making her even hotter. "But I hope so."

Her husband wasn't in the right place. Janet threw her head back and whimpered, wriggling against him.

He gave her no relief as he moved down her body, kissing and licking his way across her belly. The roaring Falls took her attention, but it rivaled the noise in her head.

Xander parted her thighs with gentle hands, his wings trembling and held high above them as he hunkered down.

Janet watched the play of moving colors as they swayed.

Until her fated mate took *all* her attention.

She screamed his name at the first swipe of his tongue, but he allowed her no recovery time, sucking her into his mouth, teasing, twirling the bundle of nerves at the top of her sex.

Janet buried her hands in his short hair, needing to hold onto something. Her hips lifted off the mattress of their own accord, but Xander gripped her, holding her down without stopping.

Pleasure crashed over her in waves. Her thighs

trembled, and she whimpered and writhed. Janet's body stiffened and she closed her eyes, letting her head fall to the soft bedding beneath her. Magic and physical ecstasy made her dizzy.

She panted, clutching at Xander's shoulders, his wings, anything she could reach. When climax made her cry out, he was there, pulling her into his chest, kissing her deeply, pushing his erection into her at the same moment.

With his first thrust, her pleasure intensified, and she moaned into his mouth. His kiss tasted different this time, mixed with her essence, but it just made Janet burn even more. She wasn't close enough to him, even with Xander moving in and out of her.

Wrapping her arms and legs around him, Janet met his next plunge, rubbing her breasts against him, encouraging him to go faster. He complied, taking her mouth again, this time harder.

Hunger washed over the bond. Whether it was his for her, or hers for him, she cared not, as long as he didn't separate from her body.

Xander stiffened above her, his erection kicking inside her as he climaxed. His orgasm brought on hers, washing over their magic as well as her form.

Janet's muscles tightened of their own accord, and she cried out.

They clung to each other as they came down, a pleasant aftershock of passion passing over her when he slipped from her core. Warmth spread across her belly, and she begged for one more kiss as Xander settled beside her.

He wrapped her in his wings for the second time, and Janet smiled against his chest. "I like how tha' feels."

Xander chuckled at her whisper. "I like how *you* feel."

Janet met that violet gaze and her head spun.

Is it magic, or something more?

She couldn't answer the question—even in her own head.

It didn't matter.

Janet MacLeod had met her match.

She was already lost to her fated mate. Her stomach flipped, and she pressed her lips to his.

chapter sixteen

The sound of rushing boots jarred Xander awake. He sat up gently, as to not disturb the lass asleep against him, and opened his eyes wider, scanning the cavern.

His heart thundered, and he couldn't take a calming breath, even though he saw nothing out of the ordinary in their hiding place.

Dim light surrounded them; he'd lessened the magic in the globes so they could sleep. Their clothing was piled haphazardly where they'd dropped it for the second night in a row.

He'd left twice, both for short trips to the Faery Stones. The first time, there'd been six winged soldiers. The second, there had only been three; Mikhias and Ruark, and a blond Fae Warrior Xander hadn't known. The two Warriors he'd stunned and questioned appeared normal.

Flying high above, with his invisibility spell in place, Xander had sensed a large warding, either intended for protection or defense—a clue that Ruark remembered and had reported their encounter.

Xander hadn't chanced getting closer, in case the spell was simply an alarm, but there was a great deal of magic packed into it. He hadn't had to touch it to feel it. To get them home, he'd have to break through it, damn the consequences, but he couldn't risk taking the time to explore unless the guard was light, and he had his wife with him.

He hadn't told Janet much upon his return to the cave, but when they were together, neither seemed to have much need for conversation. Now that he'd had her, he couldn't keep his hands off her. He'd lost count of how many times he'd taken her, in the bed and in the spring at the back of the cavern.

Xander glanced over his shoulder, spotting the steam idly rising from the pool. Almost as if it was beckoning. It was quiet.

Normal, even with the roar of the falls.

He strained his ears, but still caught nothing more of what had woken him—what had sounded like an ambush.

Was I dreaming?

Nay.

Xander's instincts screamed: *Move. Now.*

Janet made a noise in her sleep, nestling closer. The arm thrown across his waist tightened, her fingers squeezing his hip.

When he looked down, his mate's face was drawn tight, although she wasn't awake. As if she, too felt something.

Xander closed his eyes and sucked in a breath. He threw magic out into the cave, probing everything he could. He sensed no stealth magic, no warding. No protection spells or tricks.

No Fae Warriors burst into the cave, either from the side of the cliff's face, or through the rushing water.

It'd always been his talent, his gift to cast such stealth magic, as well as feel it.

Still, his gut, as well as his powers, were shouting that he needed to gather his wife up and get them away from Grànnda Falls.

This isn't magic. It's instinct.

Xander couldn't afford to question it. Even now, the hair was standing on the back of his neck.

Danger! it shouted.

"Lass." He smoothed her knitted brow. "Wake up, *mò aingeal*." He caressed her cheeks, pushing her dark hair away from her face.

Janet came around slowly, blinking as she opened her beautiful sapphire eyes. "What's wrong?" Her voice was thick with sleep, her lovely body sleep-warmed.

He wished nothing was wrong, that he could curl back up with her. Hold her, take her again. "We need to leave."

She sat up, rubbing her eyes, but when their gazes met, his wife stiffened. "Somethin's wrong."

"Aye, I think so. We need to gather our things and go."

Fright darted across Janet's face, and she latched onto his arm. "Wh-what's happenin'?"

His stomach fluttered. Xander gathered her to him, kissing her softly. "We're going home."

She pulled back, staring hard. "'Tis safe?"

"I don't know, but my gut—as well as my magic— is saying we need to move now. I can keep us invisible until we get to the dais that holds the Faery Stones. They're warded against stealth magic, but I'll get the Stones open as quickly as I'm able." He didn't tell her about the large spell he'd sensed when he'd flown overhead that morning. Xander didn't want to scare her any more than she already was, and he'd have to pray they'd get to the Stones unscathed.

Janet swallowed, but she nodded. "I trust ye."

He cupped her face, looking deep into her eyes. "I will get you home."

"Us."

"Aye, us." He nodded. Her mixed emotions hit him from the mating bond, spreading slowly across his chest and down his limbs. "All will be well, *mò aingeal*."

Once again, his wife nodded, but she made no move to pull away.

"If something happens, I need you to shut down our bond, lass."

"Wh-what?"

"You'll have to concentrate and shut me out. Push the magic away from you. We'll still be bonded—that will never go—but it will shove my feelings and emotions to the back of your mind, like an echo."

"Why, Xander?" Janet's whisper was so low he

had to strain his ears to hear her.

When her eyes misted over, Xander almost lost his nerve. However, he *couldn't*. He needed to protect her. If they were captured, death wouldn't be quick. He wouldn't be able to endure if Janet could physically feel what they were doing to him—or the reverse. The Fae would hurt his wife in the worst way possible before they killed her.

Especially if the king discovered she was a MacLeod, but worse if his uncle found out she was Alex's sister.

"It's not difficult." He cleared his throat when his voice cracked. "Picture the golden rope, gather it up, throw it away from you."

"Xander—"

"*Mò aingeal,* just tell me you'll do it, if I tell you to." Xander stroked her cheeks with his thumbs, wiping a tear away when it rolled down.

"Is it…permanent?"

After they kill me, aye.

"Nay. You can open the magic back up once we're home. It will only work at all because we've been together for such a short time. Our bond is still young, flexible. But it is still strong, as you see in the golden glow. In years to come, you won't be able to shut me out even if you're angry with me." Xander had been going for a tease, but the look on Janet's face shouted that he missed his mark.

"I've…grown used ta feelin' ye with me."

"Aye, so have I, lass. My Janey." He stared into her blue eyes.

The emotion there made his heart jump. It was echoed in the bond, and she wasn't alone in what she felt for him, though neither of them had exchanged words of affection — caring?

More?

It's been mere days.

How can I feel so much for her?

Xander didn't answer his question.

He couldn't.

The mating bond deepening was one thing.

He'd never considered it would affect him in other ways.

Which was foolish in and of itself. Mating bonds were rare, and scared most Fae, even those born with the most powerful magic.

Mating bonds were forever, and Fae could be fickle, especially with their affections.

Mating bonds could never be torn asunder. They were known to connect people at a level Xander hadn't understood until he and Janet had made love for the first time.

Bonded couples shared *everything*. Deep love. Mental and physical links that could never be replaced. Or bettered.

If either of them died, the other would soon follow — *that* scared him the most.

Janet's life literally depended on his ability to get

them back to Skye.

"Let's go home, *mò aingeal.*"

A ghost of a smile played at her lips, and she nodded.

Complete trust—among other things Xander was afraid to name—traversed the bond. Warmed him all over.

He kissed her long and hard, holding her tight against his chest for as long as he dared.

Afterward, his lass, true to her strong nature, squared her shoulders and sucked in a breath when she exited the bed, and started to dress in silence.

Xander prayed to the Goddess and the human God alike, for stealth and strength.

He had vows to carry out.

Janet had never been so scared in her life as she slung the hide bag Xander had brought from Dunvegan across her body to avoid having to hold onto the strap. Perhaps she shouldn't have arranged it as such. Then she could've clung to it with white knuckles. For now, she was fighting the urge, but her whole form shook.

He smiled when their gazes met, and if the circumstances were different, she would've melted on the spot.

Xander was *hers.*

When he closed the distance between them and

cupped her face, she met his mouth without pause. Janet took strength from him—and their bond—as they kissed. She only wished it made her feel better—or more confident—that they'd get back to Skye in one piece.

"Come, *mò aingeal*." Xander looped her arm in his and escorted her to the ledge outside the waterfall as if they were sauntering into the great hall. "Hold tight to me." He drew her into his arms and pumped the wings she'd caressed, kissed, and explored so many times in the last two days.

The bliss of being with him for the last five days had almost made her forget they were in the Fae Realm. Janet shivered. She banished her fear of heights and tried not to think of soaring high *above* the solid ground.

He squeezed her against his hard chest, as if he could read her mind—though as far as she knew he still could not. Although Xander said nothing, the move comforted. She felt it from their bond as well, and crushed her eyes shut against his shoulder as he slowly lifted into the air.

Janet's stomach somersaulted, and it had little to do with the ledge, then the falls, melting away as Xander rose higher. She still sensed in her entire being that her husband wasn't telling her everything.

The resulting helplessness didn't sit well, but she could do nothing, save pray they'd get the Faery Stones open and get back to the island where she'd grown up. Back to Dunvegan, her family's stronghold, the only home she'd ever known.

Wind buffeted her skirts and tossed her hair as her husband flew. Janet buried her face in his neck when a look down made her heart skip a beat.

Xander *believed* everything would be all right.

She felt his confidence from their mating bond. Janet needed to remember that.

The rushing air continued to be the only sound that greeted her ears. She couldn't watch the pink and purple trees when she'd tried to look around a second time, so Janet clung to her fated mate and prayed.

His flight slowed, but she didn't risk opening her eyes. Sensations prickled up and down her spine, then her limbs, all the way down to her hands and feet. Uncomfortable tingling made Janet fight the urge to shake them out, as if her fingers had fallen asleep.

Xander gasped and she lifted her head, meeting his gaze. "We've breached the spell. Are you well?"

"Spell?"

"They've cast a bubble over the area, but I cannot tell what type of magic."

When Janet looked down, she tensed.

"We're invisible; they can't see us."

They hovered high above the dais that held their only way home.

There were two Fae Warriors guarding the sacred place Xander had told her they called the Field of Light.

Although it was dark, the crystals of the magic portal glinted, giving off illumination. They were shining and rotating as if they were a white prism, and someone was turning them in sunlight.

Xander grunted and stiffened against her.

"Xander?"

He pumped his wings and they rose higher. "I want you to close your eyes when we land next to the Stones. I have to take care of Mikhias and Ruark, and I do not want you to witness violence."

"Are…ye goin' ta…kill them?"

"Only if I have to."

Janet nodded, sucking in a breath. She'd seen swordplay of course, and had had to dress training injuries, but she'd never been on a battlefield. Watching her clansmen fight in the bailey was one thing, but that was *training*. There was no real violence or tension.

"As soon as my boots touch down, my spell will be rendered useless. They'll rush us. Stay close to the Stones. I will stop the Fae Warriors and open the portal as quickly as I can."

Their eyes met and once again, she nodded. The utter surety she felt from her husband was the only thing that kept her from collapsing in his arms or giving in to the threatening tears.

He kissed her, but it was too short. Still, Janet sensed even more determination from Xander as he lowered them slowly toward the glowing Faery Stones.

She winced at the dual shout, but her husband released her and threw two blue balls of light so fast his movements were a blur. Janet squinted against the brightness, but Xander was soon back at her side, studying her face.

"Are you well, *mò aingeal*?"

"Aye," came out as a croak.

Her husband offered a curt nod. "I'm going to open the Stones. We're almost home."

As Xander dashed toward the crystal-topped pillars, she scanned the orange and blue grass.

The two Warriors were a few feet from each other, each lying in a heap of wings and limbs.

"Are they dead?" she whispered.

"Nay," he called. "Come to me, lass. When the portal opens, we must hurry."

Janet obeyed, watching as Xander touched the center crystal.

Then he tapped the other four, one after the other, as if in order. Each lit at his touch, and humming filled the air.

Wind was born from nowhere, and she shoved her hair out of her face so she could watch her husband work magic. She got nothing from the bond, except her body buzzed with an odd energy. It caused no pain but forced her to rock back and forth on her heels. It didn't feel right, but Janet didn't want to distract him, so she didn't voice the worry.

"Something's wrong." His murmur was low; she'd almost missed it with the wind rushing her ears, but her heart skipped.

"What?"

He didn't answer. Xander's hands flew over the Stones again, in the same order. Nothing changed. He did it again, slapping the crystals this time and cursing in what had to be Fae, because she couldn't translate the words to Gaelic.

Fire shot down Janet's spine, and a scream was ripped from her lips as pain came from nowhere.

Xander hollered and she fought the urge to give in when her knees buckled.

She reached for him, but her fated mate couldn't return the gesture.

His hands were glowing red, and he stood bent and frozen at the Faery Stones, his beautiful wings crumpled on his back.

Pain radiated from her limbs, but Janet fought to straighten her shoulders and tried to inch toward him.

Xander screamed her name, whipping his head back, and arching. He panted, and their gazes locked. "I cannot release the Stones. Magic holds me…burns me."

"I feel it," Janet moaned.

"Shut down our bond."

"Nay!" She shook her head. Pain shot up her arm when she grabbed his wrist, but she ignored it, trying to pull his hands from the largest crystal of the Faery Stones.

"Lass, do it. I don't want you hurting." Xander's violet eyes implored.

Janet frowned and pulled harder. Pain rebounded

from the bond, and her husband winced. His hands didn't dislodge from the crystal.

"You will not be able to free me. This was a trap. I was foolish."

A maniacal laugh filled the air, and Xander cried out.

His head fell back, but his chest heaved as if he'd sucked in a breath, and he fought to meet her eyes again.

Boot steps sounded on the stairs of the dais.

Janet froze. A whimper fell from her lips unbidden, and agony still radiated all over her whole body. She tightened her grip on Xander's wrist.

Her husband's gaze burned her face. "Run, *mò aingeal*."

chapter seventeen

Mikhias's laugh was menacing and evil. The dark-haired warrior brandished his sword as soon as he reached the top of the dais. "You cannot open the Faery Stones, no matter what you try."

The Warrior mentioned nothing about the spell that was burning its way through Xander's whole form.

He tried to extend his wings but was only presented with more pain. He couldn't straighten them or his body now and fought the fall when his muscles urged him to his knees.

"It's a trap," Xander repeated at a whisper, but his wife had still not moved from his side.

She hadn't shut the mating bond down, either. Her body was tight as she too fought the pain of the spell. Janet's sapphire eyes were wide when he met her gaze.

"Run, *mò aingeal*," he begged again, forcing each word past his lips. His tongue was thick, glued to the roof of his dry mouth as Xander tried to combat the agony with his magic. He got no response from his commands. It was worse than when he was in the Human Realm. No echo of the powers in his body. Everything was just *gone*.

Janet shook her head and clung to his arm. "Nay."

"Lass, please. You can stop your pain. Subdue the magic."

Tears rolled down her cheeks, but she glared. "Nay. I dinnae leave ye. Or be distanced from ye in any way." Her nails bit into his wrist, but it was nothing compared to the fire crippling his back, his wings.

His thighs seared as he tried to remain upright. Xander tugged but the Faery Stones only burned him more. He finally lost the battle. His legs buckled, knees hitting the planked dais with a *thud.* White-hot pain shot all the way into his torso, as if the wood was punishing him, too.

What kind of spell is this?

He was trapped, his magic gone. Xander swallowed the urge to scream. He couldn't scare his wife any more than she already was.

Foolish idiot.

It'd been too easy. He should've known something wasn't right.

He *had* felt it when they'd breached the bubble warding above the Field of Light. Xander had ignored it, sure he could overcome Mikhias and Ruark and the way home would be clear.

Wretch.

Sod.

Idiot.

The words were on a loop in his head as he battled pain unlike any he'd ever experienced.

Mikhias, with Ruark on his heels, stalked over to Janet, an evil smile spread on his lips.

Xander's stomach somersaulted, and helplessness washed over him.

I have failed Janet. Failed to protect her.

Mikhias yanked Janet away from him, and her hand slipped from Xander's wrist. She yelped as the Fae Warrior forced her to her knees.

"Unhand her. Now!" Xander's shout resulted in both Fae Warriors throwing their heads back in laughter.

"You are powerless, oh great one. Protector of no one," Mikhias barked.

"Yer wrong, my friend," Ruark said.

The dark-haired warrior frowned and threw his long plait over his shoulder. "How so?"

Ruark pointed his sword at Xander's chest. "He's a protector of traitors and humans. A poor one, at that." They both found great amusement at the redheaded Warrior's jest, laughing again, and patting each other on the shoulders. Ruark flexed his wings, but Xander looked away from the iridescent skin as his own wings ached.

Janet whimpered, and Xander strained against the invisible hold on his hands. The crystal brightened, shooting a new jolt of pain up his arms, into his biceps. His shoulders jerked of their own accord and a shudder of discomfort racked his whole frame.

Pain was etched on his wife's face, but she still

didn't push the magic that joined them away. She looked down, clutching her skirts with white knuckles.

"Do yer arms hurt, Traitor?" Ruark asked, one of his auburn brows arched.

"We could cure it. Cut them off?" Amusement rippled in Mikhias's voice.

Janet was quietly crying, but her shoulders were square, her back straight. She looked dignified, despite their situation; his respect and love for her shot up.

Love?

Warmth spread across his chest, counteracting the pain. Xander tried to block the feeling from the bond, since it was such an ill time and place to reveal his emotions, but his magic didn't respond.

However, if his wife felt it, she didn't react. Nor did she look at him. The only magic he could sense was the mating bond and the spell that held him captive.

Emptiness and pain surrounded him, except for Janet. Xander clung to it. Clung to her. He wished he could speak mentally with her. Reassure her. Tell her he loved her.

"Nay, the Captain said we do nothin' until he arrives," Ruark said.

Ice shot down Xander's spine. It should have relieved the pain, but only served to churn panic up from his gut.

My father is coming?

As if answering a mental call, Fae Warriors flew overhead in groups of twelve, full formations landing next to each other, swords drawn.

An army.

Their boots hit the orange and blue grass in line, one after another.

They stilled, holding their weapons high.

Waiting. Watching.

They would not act without command.

A great warrior, with hair as dark as midnight and a look on his face to match, landed at the center of the wings' formations. His giant sword was already drawn. His armor was gold to denote his rank.

Father.

Xander started to shake from head to toe, despite the pain raging through his body. He swallowed hard and watched the winged Fae man stalk across the orange grass.

Mikhias and Ruark fell into position, one near him, the other beside Janet, and assumed respectful expressions and poses.

Even if Xander had his magic and could read the captain's mind, he wouldn't have needed to. Fury poured off his father's huge form.

His dark hair was loose, and somehow *not* seeing it contained in a warrior braid made him even more menacing. Ebony locks flowed like an aura around him, anger infusing it, too. His armor shone brightly, bathed in magic, and lit up the area of his stride. Xander's father's magic sword was aglow. It made his already deadly skill even more sharp. Death would be the result of even a scratch from the weapon.

"Traitor," Captain Daegus boomed before his boots hit the stairs. His armor *clinked* as he ascended. It was the only sound other than Xander's rough breathing filling his ears.

"Father." Xander cursed the tremor in his voice. He couldn't blame it on pain from the spell. Even if he'd been on his feet, he would've trembled before the man's rage. At one time, fear of disappointing Captain Daegus had driven his life.

Xander had had to fight for his rank and his place among the soldiers even before he'd reached adulthood. Had had to prove himself much more so than the next Fae raised as a knight or man-at-arms. Because of the man who was glaring down at him.

"You and I share no such tie," Captain Daegus barked.

"You may have renounced me, but you can't renounce our shared blood." His voice gained strength with each word Xander pushed out of his ravaged mouth. He tried to square his shoulders, but pain darted up and down his wings. However, he didn't break eye contact with his father's yellow-gold gaze.

Captain Daegus's jaw tightened. "You are a *traitor*."

His father put magic behind the barked word, and it rocked Xander to his core.

He felt Janet's whimper more than heard it.

So did his father.

The Fae captain's eyes darted back and forth from Xander to his wife. He said nothing, but that contradictory bright-colored gaze narrowed.

He sees the bond.

Xander felt it in his gut.

"Get him away from the Faery Stones. King Fillan demands an audience with the *traitor*. Bring the lass." Captain Daegus' orders were followed without question or delay, as always.

Xander screamed when Mikhias muttered a spellword and ripped his arms from the crystal. His fingers, hands, and wrists burned all the way to his elbows, as if they were flayed open.

Agony ate him alive.

The wind that always surrounded the five crystals' magic kicked up, making Xander's skin scorch even more. He blinked and tried to focus through the pain. He expected his bones to be exposed, but when his vision cleared, he saw they were not. However, magic clung to his form, making him glow crimson. The spell hadn't ended; it'd attached itself to Xander.

Janet sobbed, hunched over on the dais, her hands covering her face, her torso shaking.

All he saw, all he could *feel* was pain. From them both.

"Lass, do it." Xander had intended to shout, but the words came out a cracked whisper.

The hilt of Ruark's sword came crashing down.

More pain burst from his forehead.

Then everything went black.

The flight to the palace wasn't with the gentle care Janet was used to in Xander's arms. The dark-haired warrior squeezed her too tightly, then dangled her precariously, laughing at her fright. Then he plastered her to the green armor of his chest-plate and fondled her breasts, squeezing them until she cried out.

Screaming seemed to excite him more, so even though he was hurting her, Janet bit her lip when she was tempted to utter her desperation. She couldn't fight him, and risk being dropped, either.

Pain racked her frame, but it was the pain her husband was feeling.

The redheaded warrior, as well as another light-haired one, flew with him in a net litter. She couldn't see Xander's face, but he was writhing against the netting, his wings bent and constricted.

Janet closed her eyes when she felt the Fae Warrior's arousal against her back. She sucked in her cheek and bit down so she wouldn't cry out.

He was going to rape her.

Her chest heaved as the idea sank in.

If she didn't push away the magic of the bond, Xander would feel her pain, like she was feeling his. Janet could endure what they might do to her, but she couldn't withstand *him* feeling it.

Her husband probably understood their intentions, but he didn't have to live through it, experience it with her.

Tears streamed down and were ripped away by the rushing air as she made the decision to distance herself from the man she was falling in love with.

The thought startled, but it was true.

Nay. Not falling.

I already love him.

Her breathing became even more difficult, and it had little to do with the Warrior's arm too-tight around her waist.

Janet loved Xander and they would both likely die without her even having a chance to tell him. She had to shut the magic down, or he would sense her feelings for him, same as whatever the Fae would do to her.

Crushing her eyes shut, she ignored the ache in her chest. She hadn't been *alone* since the moment she'd bonded with Xander.

How could she even fathom pushing away their link?

Janet hadn't known she'd needed it—needed *him*—until the bond had been born.

Her ring caught her eye. It was glowing a menacing red, as if it understood what was going on—and what she needed to do with the magic.

She ignored it. Had to endure.

'Hold Fast' is my clan dictate, is it not?

Janet pulled strength from some unknown place

and tried her best to take a deep breath. She pictured the golden rope of the bond. Her bottom lip wobbled as she imagined picking it up, as Xander had instructed. In her mind, she threw the bond away from her body. She ordered the magic's retreat, placing it to the back of her thoughts and locking it away.

Xander's pain from the spell lifted like a veil, suddenly gone; but a new—emotional—agony replaced it, making her chest burn, her heart thunder. She could already feel his withdrawal. His heart no longer beat in time with hers.

If she could have doubled over, Janet would have. Loss hit her in waves.

Her husband made a fist of the netting and hauled himself higher. He turned with an aching fragility, and even before he looked in her direction, she felt him seeking her out.

When Xander's shoulders relaxed into the litter, as if he was pleased by her decision, Janet lost the battle to fight more tears. They cascaded freely, carried away by the wind as soon as they were born.

A giant palace came into view, full of raised embattlements, turrets, and towers that sparkled in multicolors, visible in the darkness of night. Some kind of mist swirled above the actual stone, and it too glimmered.

Tremors chased each other down her spine, despite the welcoming appearance of the Fae castle, so large that Janet couldn't see the end. The place was full of dread, not comfort.

Fae were everywhere. Men-at-arms with no wings. More Fae Warriors than she could count.

Xander screamed as they set his litter on the ground and a full formation of winged Fae surrounded him.

Janet could no longer feel his pain, but seeing it was no better.

They were in some kind of training bailey, and fear settled over her as she looked around.

Fae Warriors lined all sides of the area, standing shoulder to shoulder like statues, but they all had huge swords in their grips.

The dark-haired Warrior set Janet to her feet, but he didn't release her. Ropes appeared from nowhere and he waved his fingers.

She yelped as her hands were magically bound behind her back. She fought the urge to pull away.

He winked but said nothing.

"King Fillan approaches!" someone yelled.

Silence fell.

The cruel man whom Xander had called *Father* stood by her husband as he writhed in the netting. No one had taken him out of the prison or hauled him to his feet.

The huge, winged man was dark where Xander was light, and if rage and fury hadn't flowed off him in waves, Janet would have considered him handsome. She could see her husband in his face, although their coloring was opposite.

Janet swallowed a whimper and couldn't look away from the man she loved.

How could Xander's father condone what they were doing to him?

He'd called him *traitor*.

He renounced him…

A horn sounded and she heard the rush of marching boots and clinking metal. She spotted a flag bearer first, then a Fae Warrior with a large, curved horn in his hands marching next to him.

Janet shuddered as the six armored Warriors parted, standing at attention. Instead of green armor, theirs was silver.

Fear overwhelmed her as she laid eyes on the king.

His hair was fair, but his demeanor was not. His jewel-encrusted crown sat high on his head. His white-blond locks caressed the shoulders of his royal purple robe, and the smile on his neatly trimmed bearded face chilled her blood.

She couldn't see his eyes from her distance, but Janet's gut told her they were violet, like Alana's and Xander's. However, where the two Fae she loved held warmth in their gazes, King Fillan did not.

Janet felt it. Fright made her shake from head to foot, small tremors, making their way through her body in waves. She feared the Fae king above all others.

Xander's father came forward and bowed deeply. "Your Majesty, I've found the traitor."

chapter eighteen

She cried out when they were separated. Janet couldn't help it. As soon as the king had said his piece — ordered death for them both without so much as a glance at her — he'd disappeared from the bailey with his entourage.

The Fae Warriors surrounding Xander started to beat him.

The captain watched as if detached, his glowing sword still in hand, his gold armor catching the firelight of many torches.

Some of the flames were not normal. They were blue and purple and color, but she couldn't be fascinated by it. Her situation demanded her attention remain vigilant, and on Xander.

Janet frowned. Her husband's father was evil.

Then they took Xander out of her line of sight, but she *heard* what they were doing to him.

Her scream had drawn little notice from the numerous winged Fae in the bailey.

They'd started cheering after the king had departed. Urging the cruelty on as her husband was abused.

What about his magic?

From the moment he'd touched the Faery Stones it was obvious he couldn't defend himself, but she'd seen Xander throw balls of blue light.

Why couldn't he save himself now?

"Ah, lass, looks like we're alone now," the dark-haired warrior drawled.

Panic was a living thing as rough hands pushed Janet to her knees. Her throat closed and she swallowed. She kept her eyes downcast, and her jaw locked. Her gut churned and she bit her bottom lip so hard she tasted blood.

The ropes binding her hands behind her back were tight, pain shot up into her shoulders with even the slightest shift. They must also be magic, because when Janet moved against them, they burned her flesh, like she'd touched a pot too soon after being over an open flame.

Boots came into view.

She fought tremors. Screamed at herself to stay still. Janet tried to square her shoulders, but it just hurt more. She froze in place.

"Aren't you a bonnie lass—for a human." The voice was deep, mocking.

His accent was refined in a way she'd not noticed at the Faery Stones. Each word was clear, like he thought he was better than her and wanted her to know it.

Calloused fingers yanked her face up.

Janet fought a whimper and met pale blue eyes.

They were more crystal clear than blue, like tinted ice. His warrior braid fell to his waist in a thick plait, and he was broad-shouldered. Sinfully handsome, but his expression was as frigid as the color of his eyes.

"I've never rutted a human."

Do. Not. React.

She resisted the urge to jerk away. She needed him to think she was indifferent about the whole thing.

To not *show* her fear.

Thick fingers caressed her hair and tucked loose strands behind her ear. The touch was nothing like when her husband did it.

Stay strong.

"Aye, if yer goin' ta do it, it migh' as well be now. She won't be much use for verra long," the redheaded warrior said, striding over with his sword still in hand.

"Why do you say that?" The Warrior paused, his hands still in her hair. He flexed iridescent wings.

"Can ye no' sense it? They've bonded."

"Nonsense," Ice Blue Eyes spat, frowning.

"I can see his magic all o'er her, even though we took the traitor's powers. 'Tis not a spell. A true mating bond. The captain saw it, too." The redheaded warrior tossed his braid over his shoulder.

Janet shivered.

"With a human?" The question was part fascination, part revulsion.

"Evidently not *all* human, I wouldna think." Red winked.

Janet tried not to glare. She ordered herself to maintain an apathetic expression.

"Now, I want her even more."

Tremors of fright danced up and down her spine, and she commanded herself not to strain against the magic ropes.

"As I said, do it now. When he's dead, she'll die, too. From the sounds of things," Red thumbed in the direction of Xander's latest scream, "shouldna be long now."

"Nay." The whisper fell from her lips unbidden.

Both of her captors froze.

"You care for the traitor, wee human lassie?" There was amusement in Ice Blue Eye's voice. He caressed her cheeks.

Janet's skin crawled and she fought tears.

"Aye, I think she does," Red said.

"Then I shall take her where the traitor can see. He can watch her be defiled before he dies."

Her heart stuttered. She bit back a gasp.

Red slapped Ice Blue Eyes between his wings and chuckled. "Defiled? Aren' ye a better lover than tha', Mikhias? Make her scream your name. If yer no' up to the task, I can show ye how it's done."

Her heart and stomach slid to her toes, and it took all Janet was made of to stand still and listen to the two Fae Warriors banter back and forth about raping her.

If she and Xander survived this by some miracle — or act of magic—her husband would never forgive himself if they raped her, let alone where he could see the act. Janet was glad she'd pushed the bond away. At least he wouldn't have to *feel* it.

She'd take whatever they were going to do to her without a word said and die with honor. Janet locked her fears away and grunted when Ice Blue Eyes tugged her to her feet.

Red fell in beside him and they each grabbed her upper arms.

She bit her lip to stave off a scream when her husband came into view.

Xander was in the center of six warriors chanting magic, the word *traitor*, and kicking him in time.

His father was now missing from the bailey.

"Turn him this way!" Red hollered.

"The lass is his mate. They've bonded," Ice Blue Eyes said. "He needs to watch while I take her."

Janet averted her eyes, but not before she caught Xander stilling on the ground. No doubt he'd heard the order and declaration.

Two Fae Warriors grabbed Xander and hauled him to legs that wouldn't hold his weight. They propped him up between them; one held his head so he couldn't look away.

Ice Blue Eyes chuckled and dragged two fingers down Janet's cheek, but he was looking at Xander. "Look while I touch your mate, Traitor. I'll make her scream my name."

"Then she'll scream mine," Red chimed in.

Murmurs of encouragement went through the group that held Xander captive.

Janet winced when Ice Blue Eyes licked his lips.

He tore at her bodice, making her body sway as he loosened the ties and ripped it off.

She locked her jaw and fought the threatening tears. Kept her eyes straight ahead, because she couldn't look at the man she loved, and she *wouldn't* look at the man about to rape her.

Ice Blue Eyes tore her leine as he tried to get it off her.

Red helped him with her skirts, and soon dark wool pooled at her feet.

Trembling started; Janet couldn't stop it no matter how hard she tried.

When they pulled her chemise off her body, and the night air hit her bare form, she lost the battle with her tears.

They spilled over, clouding her vision. She sank her teeth into her bottom lip again. Janet tugged against the magic ropes binding her hands to no avail. She wanted to run, but if she did, they would probably be even rougher with her. She wouldn't resist. Hopefully it would be quick.

Red whistled. "The lass is beautiful, human or not."

"Perfect," Ice Blue Eyes breathed.

She stood before them naked as the day she was born but squared her shoulders despite the tightness of the ropes. Janet mustered a glare.

Red chuckled. "Fire in this one, Mikhias. Careful now."

A shuffling sound drew her attention and Janet's eyes shot to her husband.

Xander was struggling against his captors, pain etched his bloody face. His mouth moved, but no sound fell out.

Her stomach somersaulted and she wanted to call out that it would be all right, despite what they did to her. Janet wanted to beg him to close his eyes.

So, they both wouldn't have to endure him watching it.

She whimpered as the winged soldiers released their holds on him.

Her husband tumbled to the dirt, and they started kicking him.

After the audible rush of air puffed from his mouth, Xander lay still—much too still, but they didn't stop kicking him.

A sob fell from her mouth, and she stared, begging him to be alive.

Ice Blue Eyes grabbed her jaw and wrenched her face to his. His mouth bruised hers.

The kiss was over before she could bite him. His fingertips brushed her bare breasts, and she cried out.

"You'll like it with me, lass." His breath hit her cheek and Janet's gut tightened. She wished she could vomit on command.

"Enough!" The roar shook the bailey as Xander's father landed hard, dust flying up over his gold armor and iridescent wings. He stalked between the two groups of Fae, drawing his glowing sword.

All the winged warriors froze.

Janet shuddered.

"Take the lass to the dungeons. Do. *Not.* Touch. Her. The traitor has had enough. Take him away. Even he deserves reprieve before execution."

The word made Janet quiver even more.

Consciousness roared in and out in crushing waves. Xander's body pulsed with a crippling agony that kept him pinned to the holey pallet in the dank cell. He pressed against the stone wall because it was cool and offered some relief to his swollen face, though it, too, hurt.

He couldn't judge how long he'd been in the dungeons.

Ribs were broken, eyes swollen shut and he couldn't straighten his wings, or his limbs. His right arm was broken and rested across his torso, throbbing. One of his wings was torn.

If Xander had any blood left in his veins, it wasn't much.

Still had no access to his magic, but the burning spell had been lifted.

Now he was mostly numb, his body's defense to too much stimulus.

Janet…

Xander couldn't feel her. She was the barest echo in his mind.

He'd wanted her—begged her—to shut down the bond, but now that she had—loss was as crippling as physical agony.

The bastards had raped her.

A sob ripped from his lips against his will.

Failure.

Xander had failed her—his mate, the most important female to him—in the *worst* way possible. He didn't know when it'd happened, but suddenly his cousin, the princess he'd sworn to give his life for, if necessary, was no longer his primary concern.

Janet is — was.

"I don't deserve her."

It was a good thing she'd pushed the bond away. He couldn't bear what she must be feeling now. Janet must loathe him as they both waited for death.

She was a smart lass. She'd trusted him. Would know how horribly he'd failed her.

Janet would never forgive him.

Should never forgive him.

Once his father killed him, she would die within weeks, unless her human blood affected the severed bond differently. Regardless, she'd never see her family again.

Everything is your fault.

Her blood is on your hands.

"Open this cell. Move aside. I was sent to heal the traitor." A familiar voice scrambled the chaos in his mind.

Xander trembled on the straw pallet, but his eyes wouldn't open when he tried. He lay on his side and could do no more than rock back and forth. New jolts of pain shot into his legs, so he made himself lie still.

Heal me?

Why?

Probably so they could torture him again before his death sentence was carried out. King Fillan had instructed his father to deal the final blow. Captain Daegus, ever obedient, agreed.

To kill his only child.

The crystal bars brightened when the lock-spell was released, Xander sensed more than saw. He heard the rustling of fine fabric.

Her gasp was full of emotion, which confirmed her identity, but only confused him more.

Mother?

"Leave us," she commanded. The words shook.

"I've orders to remain with the traitor until the change of guard, Lady Aileana," a deep voice responded.

"I need to concentrate. Lock me inside. I shall call you when I'm through. He will not hurt me."

There was some grumbling, but booted feet soon

retreated.

"Oh, my lad, my Xander." Her voice was anguished, and soft hands cupped his face.

He groaned; if his mouth could've opened, Xander would have cried out, as the touch shoved pain all the way to his ears.

She sniffled as she muttered nothings, but he heard spellwords, too. Moisture hit his cheeks. His mother was crying as she healed him. Her touch was warm, but he couldn't yet see the glow that accompanied healing magic.

Agony started to recede from his face. Heat spread down his neck, covering his shoulders and torso. Soothing, brushing him like a dozen warm caresses, lifting the hurts and aches and sharp pains.

Xander grunted as his ribs knitted and his arm straightened of its own accord when the bone was once again whole. Pain melted from his torn wing, too.

He blinked until his vision cleared but had to squint against his mother's glowing form. Now that his eyes were no longer sealed shut, any bit of light was like a new assault; he needed his sight to adjust.

Healing magic was bright white light. Her aura was bathed in it as she worked. She was powerful, so not even a bead of sweat was born on her brow. Her hands traveled his form as she chanted the words to empower and strengthen his body.

Xander watched in silence, emotion catching in his throat.

The last time he'd seen her she'd been in bed, surrounded by the fog of Acana root, and it hadn't been long before he'd fled the realm with Alana and the MacLeods.

Who was this ethereal creature, with her loose white-blonde locks falling to her waist and body clad in the finest lavender gown?

The hue spoke of her former royalty, and the gown was elegant, with jewels sown into the bodice.

The final pressure of his wounds lifted, and her radiance started to fade. When their eyes met—hers were violet, a match for his own—his mother smiled, and Xander's heart skipped. Gone were the red-rimmed eyes and unnaturally pink stained cheeks of Acana root addiction.

"*Màthair*," he whispered in Fae.

"My lad." Her smile was brilliant now and she cupped his face, her eyes raking up and down. "Do you hurt anywhere?"

Xander shook his head. "*Màthair*?"

"Aye?"

"*Màthair*?" His repetition caused a low laugh, and she helped him sit up.

As soon as Xander was upright, she threw her arms around him.

So many words whirled through his head, but nothing would come out of his mouth. He hugged the slight, delicate Fae woman who'd given him life. It was only the third or fourth time he'd ever been embraced by her, if memory served.

"There is so much I want to tell you," she said. Like him, his mother was a mind reader. She had no doubt plucked the questions from his head. "And no time to do so. We need to get your lass and go."

"Go?"

"Aye, my lad. I'm here to get you out."

chapter nineteen

"I shall call the guard. Can you knock him out?" Lady Aileana's voice was low and urgent.

Xander backed out of her embrace and stood, stretching his wings and his spine. He shook out his arms and legs. "Aye. My magic has returned."

"Good. Stay in the shadows, against the wall. I shall tell him I put you to sleep. He knows I'm your mother, of course. He'll think I did you a kindness."

"Before I'm put to death," Xander spat the words, unable to hold back his bitterness.

She fell silent. "Aye." The word was shaky.

"Mother, they'll kill you for this."

"Nay. Your father will protect me. We've a plan, my lad. I am here because my Daegus could not risk it. Do not worry for either of us."

Shock rolled over Xander, and his throat went dry. "Father?"

"Aye."

He had no time for a retort.

His mother called for the guard. The shuffling of boots and magic keys greeted his ears, but it did nothing to prevent the emotion that constricted his chest.

His father was behind the unexpected rescue?

Hadn't the man been ready to deliver his death blow?

"All is well, Lady Aileana?"

"Aye, he is resting. Healed, as ordered. I must see to the human lass. Where is she?" The former princess' voice was steady. Sure.

Xander needed to trust his parents' plan.

Janet.

His stomach fluttered and he fought a tremor. He couldn't face his wife. He'd been the cause of her rape.

I don't deserve her.

At least his mother was going to ensure what he'd failed to do—get Janet home.

Magic bound them for life, but perhaps if she kept the bond distanced—and neither of them invited it back, Xander could retreat.

She needed someone who matched her.

Could protect her.

Not a failure like him.

He made himself focus on what the man-at-arms was telling his mother.

The oversized guard opened the cell, the crystal bars catching in the blue and purple flamed torches that lined the dungeon corridor.

Xander called to his magic, forming a blue ball of fire—a blast spell—and flinging it at the guard. He hit him square in the chest; the guard crumpled to the filthy rushes with a *thud*.

"Quickly, drag him inside," his mother urged. "Get his keys."

He did her bidding, and they locked the unconscious guard in Xander's dungeon cell.

"We need to get the lass and get to the Stones under the light of the moon. We haven't much time; morning is not so far off. Your father told me you're mated to her. I felt the magic when I healed you. I am happy for you, my lad. You love her. I just hope to see you to the Human Realm in safety."

"I failed her." Misery coated his voice even to his own ears, but Xander didn't fight his mother's delicate hand on his forearm. He reeled over all the thoughts that she revealed. Things he did not want to hear out loud. Xander built walls in his mind so she could not read anything else.

Lady Aileana gave him a squeeze. "Worry about nothing but getting out of here alive. You can never return, my lad. Whatever possessed you?"

He heard no censure or judgment. Just a worried concern that made awareness tingle down his spine.

She might have been absent for most of his childhood, but she did love him. In the back of his mind, Xander had always known that.

Perhaps it was why he'd kept returning to her, checking on her, and hoping that she would overcome her addiction. Obviously, she had.

"The ring pulled Janet into the realm. I only sought to get her and return."

"Ah. It matched you. Its job was done, so it tried to come home. A spell of your father's mother, no doubt."

Xander nodded. "As Alana suspected."

His mother tilted her head up to meet his eyes. "How is my niece?"

"Blissfully happy. Expecting again."

Lady Aileana smiled, and her beauty stunned him. She looked years younger.

His heart thumped. *"Màthair..."*

"I'll explain on our journey, my lad. I can read your questions, but we must retrieve your mate." She wretched a supply closet open at the end of the corridor. "Put this on, cover your head."

"A monk's robe?"

"'Tis large enough to cover your wings. We'll tell the guards you're performing the human's death rites."

The word *death* in conjunction with his wife shook Xander all over, but he obeyed, pinning his wings to his back, and slipping into the thick black wool. He yanked up the hood, tilting his head down and holding his hands clasped in front of his middle, as a Fae holy man would.

They arrived at her cell in silence. His mother cajoled the guard, and Xander stunned him with another blast spell.

He couldn't look at Janet as Lady Aileana introduced herself.

When she saw him, his wife gasped and threw herself into his arms, but his own only lifted to return her embrace automatically. He didn't deserve to hold her, although his heart leapt when she squeezed him closer.

Janet quivered against his chest and his gut clenched. The first sob greeted his ears and Xander struggled to hold himself together.

He burned to comfort her, whisper sweet nothings, and stop the trembling. Rub her back. Tell her all would be well.

Tell her he loved her.

He didn't deserve her.

He was the cause of all her pain.

"Xander," Janet whispered.

"Lass."

Her gaze scanned his face in the dimness, but he averted his eyes. He could feel nothing from the bond, of course, but in his peripheral vision, Xander caught her frown.

Janet swiped at the tears on her cheeks, her dark brow knitted. Hurt dominated her expression.

"Come, we must flee," his mother whispered.

Janet whimpered when he gently dislodged from her arms.

Xander wanted to cup her cheeks and kiss her, but why would she want to touch her lips to his, the man that'd failed her so badly?

After what had happened, how could she bear his touch at all?

The word *rape* reverberated in his mind, and his

throat started to close.

His wings shook, then his shoulders, his arms, and tremors racked his torso. He fought the urge to sob or double over, and bit down until his gums ached. He cleared his throat and made himself meet his mother's eyes. "You needn't risk it. Thank you for freeing us, but I can take us the rest of the way."

"Nay. I need to guide you through the tunnels. We will spill into the woods, and I shall open the Faery Stones."

Although he was familiar with the tunnels because of his many adventures with his cousin, he didn't voice that. His mother could open the portal in minutes, unlike the time it would take him. It would be foolish to refuse the offer of her assistance.

Xander's heart sped up. A sense of inadequacy washed over him, and he could feel Janet's stare. She was silently begging him for eye contact. Instinct told him so, although he couldn't sense it through magic.

"Come, this way," Lady Aileana urged.

Janet slipped in front of him, he behind her, as his mother took a turn down a winding corridor of the dungeons.

As bodyguard to the princess, he was familiar with the many escape tunnels beneath the vast palace, but his mother was taking them in a direction he'd never been.

They moved in silence and darkness. The faster they went, the more the black robe constricted. Xander shoved the hood back but didn't take the time to whip it off.

Sooner than he'd expected, the tunnel narrowed. Air whistled, rustling his hair.

"Almost there," his mother whispered, her voice bouncing off the rounded stone walls.

Janet tripped over a root as soon as they entered one of the many forests surrounding the palace.

Xander darted forward, shooting his arm around her waist to keep her on her feet.

"Thank ye," she said.

He nodded. Touching her was a bad idea. It only made him want to do it again. Hold her. Kiss her.

"My lad, you must fly us. Your father arranged a gap that will be seen as a misunderstanding in the schedule. The Faery Stones will only be unguarded until the sun is up; we've not much time."

"Aye." Xander whipped the robe up and off, stretching his cramped wings even before the wool hit the bright yellow grass at their feet.

"Come close," his mother urged when Janet hesitated.

He ventured a look at the tree canopy. It was still dark but fading fast. Dawn would be greeting them soon — too soon.

The two women pressed close and Xander tucked them into his chest. His mother was petite and slight, like his cousin, and barely came to his chest. His wife was taller, her head almost to his shoulder. She was curvy and perfect.

Both were dear to him, although he regretted not knowing more of his mother as she was now, with clear violet eyes and a sharp mind.

"I am better because of you, my lad," she whispered as she read his mind.

He hadn't taken time to reinforce his thought-blocking.

Janet said nothing, but watched with somber wide eyes as Xander pumped his wings.

When they were airborne, his mother cast a bubble spell, enclosing them from the wind, as well as making them invisible. She'd be able to speak without the wind taking away her words.

"I grieved when you left, but after learning the reasons Alana fled, I understood why you had to go. So did your father, despite his public renouncement. He had to say those things for the benefit of my brother. But your father grieved you, too."

Xander tried not to scoff and took them higher. His father had never treated him anything other than just another soldier in his rankings.

"No, lad. Your father truly loves you."

"He has an odd way of showing it."

"As did I when you were wee. Neither of us raised you as we should've." His mother's voice was bathed in regret. "I cannot go back and fix my mistakes, but this I can do for you. *We* can do this for you."

"Father will protect you?" Xander's voice cracked.

Despite everything, he loved his parents as they loved him.

"Aye. He's a plan to wipe memories. It shall be as if you were never here."

Xander clenched his jaw. It was not unheard of, but very difficult, given how many Fae they'd interacted with. He prayed to the Goddess his father could do it, and he wasn't leaving his parents only to have them slaughtered. He would never know, either.

"All will be well, my lad."

Janet whimpered and hid her face against his neck as the Field of Light came into view.

Xander tightened his arm around her, but his mother was the one to offer comfort.

"All will be well for you both. You shall be back in your realm within moments."

His wife nodded.

They landed on the dais and his mother muttered a cleansing spell. "We must hurry; the wards have been renewed, as well as the alarms."

Xander wanted to gather Janet back to him when she slipped from his arms, but he contented himself with standing beside her.

Lady Aileana darted to the Faery Stones, saying another spell to nullify the tamper alarm. It wouldn't last long.

The Stones hummed as she touched them in order, and the wind was soon born, along with the first *pop*.

Janet trembled as her skirt shifted and she inched

closer to him.

Xander reached for her, chiding himself because he couldn't help it, but she entwined their fingers and squeezed as if she needed his touch.

The portal was born, the round window-like magic opening painfully slowly.

His heart thundered when the haziness took too long to clear.

"You must go," his mother said. Her eyes were misty as she joined them.

Xander's stomach jumped. "I will miss you, *Màthair*."

Janet released him so he could hug his mother.

He held her close, kissing her forehead.

She reached up, cupping his face. "Be happy, my lad."

"You as well, *Màthair*."

"I am once again, with your father. My Daegus." Her smile was dreamy, like a young lass. "We still love each other, after all these years."

Xander couldn't imagine the hard Fae captain loving anyone—let alone showing it—but he prayed her words were true. That his parents had come to peace with each other. Found happiness he'd never been witness to as a lad.

They weren't fated mates, but had bound themselves in magic, an irreversible oath spell that must've been torture for them both while all was not well in their marriage—for years.

He nodded, mixed emotions churning in his gut.

Lady Aileana hugged his wife and whispered something that made Janet nod.

Janet came to his side quickly, and he allowed her to take his hand again.

Xander was the one to entwine their fingers this time. He pulled her closer to his side. His eyes grazed their freedom.

Because the Faery Stones were in a cave, darkness dominated the doorway into the Realm of the Humans, but Skye was only two steps away.

They'd come out on the beach; Alana's spells would prevent them from entering the realm in the cave.

"Home," Janet whispered.

Hand in hand, they walked through the portal.

chapter twenty

Something was *wrong*. He wouldn't look at her; he winced every time she reached for him. Even now, with their fingers entwined, Xander was holding back from Janet.

When they'd stepped through the portal, they were on the beach of Skye.

She recognized the large boulder she'd tried to cling to before being sucked into the Fae Realm.

Her husband's wings were gone again. He'd made a face of pain, but when she'd asked if he was physically hurting, Xander had told her he was fine.

Dawn arrived, the sun shy as it greeted the day, hiding behind fat white clouds. It was chilly, too.

Xander's retreat was the reason for her tremors, not the wind that shifted her hair.

Janet stumbled, like she had in the forest, and he steadied her again. Her heart sank when he released her. "Thank ye," she whispered.

"You're welcome, lass."

Lass. Not angel.

For the second time.

Hurt washed over her as Xander looked down the beach, away from her.

It was jarring seeing him without wings, even though over the time she'd known him, Janet had seen him without them more than she had seen him with them. She grown used to the iridescent appendages and missed them.

Maybe that's what's bothering him, despite what he said?

"Are you well?" she whispered.

He didn't pause his stride, nor did he meet her eyes, even when she tugged on his hand.

"Aye."

"Yer...magic? Do ye mourn yer wings?" she pressed.

"I'm well." Xander smiled, but it was forced.

Janet's mouth went dry, and she sniffled. Loss hit her chest, and spread, making it ache. "Xander..." She wanted to reach for him, because he'd broken their physical contact, but she didn't.

A shout went up, ripping her attention from the man she loved.

Her brothers ran toward them, Duncan's plaid whipping in the wind as he jogged.

Alex was on his heels, and her nephew behind his father, running on much shorter legs.

Her father stood on the ridge, waving vigorously. Even in the distance, she could see his grin.

Duncan reached them first, sweeping her to him in a hard hug.

Alex was next, embracing her with more care and

kissing her cheek.

Janet laughed when Angus threw his arms around her waist and squeezed.

"Aunt Janet! Aunt Janet!" the lad chanted.

She ruffled his dark hair and held him tight, dropping a kiss on the top of his head. Angus was already getting tall; he was but ten, and yet almost to Janet's shoulders. No doubt he would be the same size as his father and uncle when he grew up.

"Lass, are ye well? Hale?" Alex asked. Her laird brother offered a tentative smile, but his blue eyes were assessing.

She didn't want to look at him anymore.

Duncan cupped her face, his gaze searching. "Yer home."

"Aye, I'm hale. Home." Janet plastered on a smile for her brothers, but she felt Xander retreat even further, and bit her lip so she wouldn't give in to the urge to cry.

"Welcome home, brother." Alex, ever the diplomatic one, threw his hand out to Xander and gave him a hard shake.

"Thank ye fer bringing our sister home," Duncan echoed, patting him on the shoulder. "Now I can call ye brother."

Janet sucked in her cheek and blinked.

Xander smiled, but it was strained.

If her brothers noticed, they didn't react.

Angus left her side to embrace Xander, and at least

her husband accepted the lad's affection and returned it.

Something is still wrong.

Janet needed to be alone with him so they could talk.

Dread and loss churned in her belly.

They were home.

Should this not be a joyous occasion?

"Come, come. Alana is anxious to see ye both," Alex said.

"Come ta me, lass," their father called from the ridge. "I've yet to see ye!"

Janet obeyed, hugging her father when she reached his side.

"I'm glad yer home safe, Janey." Iain MacLeod's blue eyes were misty, and her father's smile was warm and gentle on his bearded face.

When he pulled her into a hug, she had to hold onto him for a little bit longer than she'd embraced either of her brothers. In that moment, she needed her da.

Janet smiled when she slipped from the older man's arms, and it was genuine, but the childhood nickname only made her think of when Xander called her by it.

The retired laird studied her face, his brow knitted, but she avoided his blue eyes, just like she had Alex's.

"Let's go home!" Angus pumped his arm with his shout, and the men chuckled.

She could've kissed her nephew for the distraction.

Her family was smothering her. Again.

Janet dislodged from all the hugs and love, her eyes searching her husband out.

Xander hugged his cousin, but then stayed in the corner whilst everyone fussed over them both.

"Everything okay?"

She tore her gaze away from Xander, meeting Claire's green eyes. Forced yet another smile. "Aye. Glad to be home."

Her sister-by-marriage rubbed her distended tummy and nodded. "I'm glad. I missed you. And Duncan was beside himself with worry."

"He dinnae need ta fash. I was with Xander."

Claire smiled. "I know. I trusted he'd bring you home. Are you excited about the wedding?"

Janet reared back. "Wedding?"

A blush lit Claire's high cheekbones. "Uh oh…" Her sister-by-marriage shifted on her feet. "Um, I guess no one told you? Mairi and Alana planned everything. Even had a gown made. It's tomorrow. I probably wasn't supposed to spill the beans."

Even after the almost seven months Claire had been in their time, some of her phrasing was still hard to understand. Janet let the words process until she got the meaning. "Nay, 'tis fine. Perfect." She prayed her words, were not as rushed as they sounded to her ears.

Or, it would be perfect, if everything was right with Xander.

She smiled because she didn't like the way Claire was looking at her.

"You sure you're okay? You're flushed. Maybe you should take a bath and get some sleep."

"I'm well, but tha' sounds heavenly."

Claire visibly relaxed. "Good. I'll have Mairi order you a bath."

"Nay, nay, I'll do it." Movement caught her attention, and Janet spotted Xander slip from the room. "I will see ye a' midday meal." She hurried out of the solar without waiting for Claire's answer.

He ignored her first call to him in the corridor.

Janet jogged to catch up, following him into his quarters.

Her husband whirled on her when she shut the door with a *thud*, a slam she'd not intended.

"You shouldn't be here. Your brother will kill me," Xander said.

"I dinnae be concerned abou' Duncan. I'm concerned about ye. And me."

"All is well."

"Nay. It dinnae be so, and ye well ken it. Talk ta me, Xander." Janet took two steps into the room, but he moved away.

Her fated mate reared back as if she'd hit him.

"Lass—"

"Dinnae shut me out. We're home. We can wed an' move on with our lives." Her ring glowed a pale blue, as if it agreed.

Her husband fell silent, but he closed his eyes.

Although she felt nothing but an echo from the bond, she could sense his pain.

Janet closed the distance between them and reached for his hand. Hurt rebounded back when he pulled away. "Xander, wha'—?"

"How can you *want* to touch me?" Xander's fair brows were drawn tight, a frown marring his handsome face.

"What?" It was Janet's turn to frown.

"After—" His voice broke on the word, and it dawned on her what he was referring to.

Xander had passed out when she'd been naked in front of the two Fae Warriors.

Before his father had stormed into the bailey.

"They dinnae rape me."

His violet gaze searched her face. He said nothing.

"They dinnae. I promise."

She'd expected relief, but he didn't show any. Janet wished the bond was open, so she could get a sense of what he was feeling. She got no clues from his expression.

"I should've protected you."

"Ye did. Ye got us home."

Xander's mouth was a hard line. He shook his

head and took a step back, averting his violet eyes.

"I dinnae understand," she whispered.

"You should just…go."

Hurt and anger boiled up from Janet's gut. "Ye pushed me away in the dungeon when all I wanted was ye. All I could see was ye. *Ye* hurt me more than they could have. Over somethin' ye *assumed*. Mayhap ye shoulda asked *me* instead a' pushin' me away." She waited for him to answer, but when he still wouldn't look her way, she planted her hands at her sides so she wouldn't smack him.

"I failed you." The words were so low she almost missed it.

Her stomach flipped. "Dinnae I be the judge a' tha'?"

"Nay. I shall."

"Yer throwin' *us* away, fer some weak self-pity?"

Xander winced but didn't defend himself.

Desperation hit her in waves. She *refused* to lose the man she loved over some misplaced sense of pride. However, she wasn't ready to put words to him aloud, either. Not when he wouldn't look her in the eye.

Janet pictured the golden mating bond. She imagined picking it up, holding it close, clung to the memory of seeing it disappear into her chest, watching it do the same to Xander. She sucked in a breath and called the magic to her, feeling warmth rush her chest, envelope her like when they'd bonded.

Then she focused on Xander, mentally offering

him the bond, throwing it at him in her mind.

Her husband's violet eyes went wide. He shook his head.

He's rejecting me.

Rejecting our bond.

Pain crashed down, squeezed Janet's chest, and stole her breath. "Nay," she whispered. "*Ye* said we were fated. *Ye* said we were meant ta be. *Ye* said ye dinnae fight this. What a' yer vow now?"

"It's better this way, lass." Misery saturated Xander's voice, but she didn't care.

"Lass? I thought I was yer angel?"

The apple of his throat bobbed, his lips parted, but he didn't speak.

A sob threatened but Janet wouldn't cry in front of him. "Ye care nothin' fer me?"

She waited for what felt like a lifetime.

Still the man who was supposed to be *hers* for the rest of their lives said nothing.

Janet swallowed, but she couldn't keep the tears at bay.

She fled his room, where she shouldn't have been alone with him in the first place.

Janet ran down the corridor, seeking her own room, not stopping when Duncan called her name. She passed the solar, and the laird's ledger room, finally reaching the solace of her chamber. She slammed the door and leaned on it, her chest heaving from agony, as well as the sprint.

The gorgeous pale blue wedding gown laid out on her bed, right on top of the MacLeod tartan, made her heart ache. The fabric shimmered in the sunlight streaming in through the window.

Tears fell freely and her vision blurred.

Suddenly her rooms weren't any place she wanted to be.

How could fate have failed me so badly?

chapter twenty-one

The knock on the door jarred her awake, and Janet rolled over in bed. The sun was no longer streaming into her rooms. She must've cried herself to sleep…hours ago? She was on her feet with the second knock, and her stomach fluttered.

Xander?

"Janet?"

Her heart sank as the door opened.

The last person she wanted to see was her sister-by-marriage.

Alana entered the room without permission but took one look at Janet and froze just inside. Her violet eyes were wide. "What's wrong?"

"Nothin'."

The former princess shook her head. "Magic, remember? I feel your pain. Your sense of loss. What did Xander do?" Her fair brows were drawn tight, and her irritation at her cousin was obvious.

For some reason, Janet wanted to defend him. "Nothin'." Repetition did nothing to clear Alana's expression.

"I came to see if you liked your wedding gown." Her sister-by-marriage pointed to the dress, which was balled up on a chair by the fireplace.

"Dinnae look like I'll be needin' tha'." She swallowed the sob that accompanied her words.

Alana frowned, straightening the pale blue shimmery gown, and laying it on Janet's bed. "What are you talking about? Tell me what happened."

She shook her head.

Her sister-by-marriage sat on the bed and patted an open space of MacLeod tartan beside her.

Janet's body responded against her will, and before she knew it, Alana had slipped an arm around her waist and squeezed.

"I love him," she blurted. Tears formed and spilled. She sniffled, but more flowed.

Alana rubbed her arm. "I can feel it. And I'm so glad."

"He dinnae want me anamore."

"What?" Her sister-by-marriage's eyes flashed.

Janet launched into everything that'd happened when they were in the Fae Realm. She omitted their lovemaking, but Alana was astute. Probably wouldn't fool her.

The former princess winced when she retold the near-rape and shared her astonishment regarding Xander's parents helping them escape.

When she explained subduing the bond, and Xander declaring how he'd failed her, Alana wore a scowl like none Janet had seen before.

"I shall have a word with him," the former

princess said, as if she was announcing a royal decree.

Embarrassment hit Janet and she pulled away from the comfort of Alana's arm, grasping both of her hands and tugging. "Nay. Please…just leave it. I'll…be well, given time." Speaking the thought, made her want to crumble. She would never be well. Because she loved him too much.

"Mating bonds do not operate like that, sister."

"What?"

"You can shut the magic out, but only for so long. Subduing is the same as denying. You will both be miserable, perhaps physically sick."

Heat crept up Janet's neck and she averted her gaze. "We…consummated tha bond."

Alana's low laugh had her meeting violet eyes she wanted to avoid, because they were too much like Xander's. "I figured as much."

Janet's cheeks burned even more.

"Don't fash overmuch, I won't tell Alex, let alone Duncan. 'Tis none of their concern. However, *neither* will take to postponing the wedding."

Her heart skipped. "I dinnae want ta postpone it. I want ta be his wife," Janet whispered.

Alana's smile was soft, empathetic. "You already are, sister."

"I dinnae be Fae. My brothers—an' my father— dinnae accept that. We need a priest."

"Aye, I know it. We'll have one. He's to arrive tonight. The wedding and the feast are all planned for the morrow."

"I dinnae have a husband." Sorrow crashed down over her when she spoke the sentence that hurt the most. Janet's shoulders caved in. She couldn't sit up straight because she was in too much pain.

"Yet, you don't want me to speak to my cousin?"

"I dinnae want his hand forced." Janet's voice broke. She wiped her face.

Alana hugged her tightly. "But, sister, fate has already done so. The two of you belong together — quite literally."

"Weel, if only Xander agreed."

Her sister-by-marriage's mouth set in a determined line Janet didn't like.

"Please dinnae speak with him," she implored, squeezing the former princess' hands.

"I'll see you at evening meal. Come down to the great hall." Alana rose from the bed and inclined her head. She ignored Janet when she called her name, shutting the door quietly.

"I'm goin' ta kill him. Move out a' my way. I dinnae want ta have ta contend wit' my brother if I move ye myself, Alana."

"I'm taking care of this, Duncan." His cousin's firm voice made Xander snort.

Once a princess, always a princess.

She'd sounded so sure and regal.

Dinner had been a horrid affair full of glares from the MacLeod twins. They probably didn't know what exactly had happened between him and Janet, but they knew all was not well. They'd seen his wife crying, no doubt.

Xander should tell Alana to allow their brother-by-marriage into his room. Death would be a blessing.

Nay. Then I'll fail her even more.

His magic—and his wings—were gone again. Except for his dreaded mind reading ability, of course.

He wasn't trying to read Duncan MacLeod's mind, but the man's thoughts were loud and dark—all pointed at harming him.

Xander had been torn bare. Vulnerable in a way *other* than the hurt concerning his fated mate. He'd lied to Janet when he'd denied mourning his wings.

He was trapped in the Human Realm.

"Alana—" Duncan's voice was full of warning.

"Give me a moment, Duncan. Please."

The large man uttered what sounded like a growl, but soon Xander heard the door to his quarters shut—his brother-by-marriage on the other side.

"Xander, I never thought I'd have to call you a fool, but you are *worse* than that, cousin." Alana whirled on him, hands on her hips. Gone was the false calm she'd offered Duncan. Her violet eyes flashed, and a scowl marred her pretty face. "You march down that hall, tell that lass you're sorry and assure her you'll be at your wedding on the morrow."

"Wedding?" Mixed emotions hit him in the chest, and he fought the urge to crush his eyes shut.

That explains the presence of the priest.

"Aye. Did you not see Father Bartholomew in the hall? Mairi and I have it all planned. As a surprise for you both, as well as to appease Duncan and Alex, because I know damn well Janet is no longer a maid." Her un-princess-like curse should've jarred him, but it didn't. It wasn't often his cousin said such things.

Xander mustered a smirk. "How are you so sure?"

Alana gave him a long look. "She told me. Besides, I sense the completed bond. But shutting out magic is not good. It feels wrong, Xander."

He waved his hand. It wasn't often he didn't want his cousin's company, but this was one of those times. He just wanted her to leave him alone. However, placating Alana had never worked, but he could try. "All is well."

"All is *not* well. My sister-by-marriage is sobbing. My cousin, her *fated* mate, has rejected her. What if she carries your child?"

Xander startled. "Does she? Your magic can sense it."

Alana frowned. "I have not tried to sense it. It does not matter, cousin. You're crushing her heart."

"Her heart?" He closed his eyes. If his cousin's empathic magic had sensed something, he didn't want to know.

"*Your* heart," Alana whispered. "You love her." His cousin's voice was breathless.

Xander was grateful she said nothing of his wife's feelings. Of his own, there was no use denying. "Aye."

Empathy glowed from her violet gaze as she took a seat beside him on the bed. "Then why are you doing this?"

"I don't deserve her." His voice broke, so Xander cleared his throat. "I failed to protect her."

"Foolish man," Alana spat, but there was more sympathy in her tone than venom.

"What did she tell you?"

"Everything, Xander. She's fine. She doesn't hold any concerns about what happened. Janet just wants to marry you."

"I…" Xander's heart leapt but he tried to ignore it.

His cousin pursed her lips. "You cannot live forever with a rejected bond."

"We solidified it."

"Aye, but you can still get weak. Sick."

Xander shook his head.

Alana squeezed his forearm. "Go. Tell her you love her. Marry her. Set the bond—and your marriage—right, cousin."

He averted his eyes, studying the stone floor around his boots.

She sighed. "I wish you weren't a soldier."

"What?"

"You have stupid notions of pride that do not

matter. I understand it's who you are. And your sense of duty is one of the many reasons I love you, but it also makes you a *fool*. Because you cannot move past your own failures — or what *you* see as a failure —"

"Alana —"

His cousin put a palm up. "Let me finish."

Xander frowned but nodded.

Alana took a breath. "You found your fated mate. The lass you're supposed to be with for the rest of your life. You fell in love with her. That is all that matters."

"It's not."

"It is."

"I failed in my duty as her mate to protect her."

"She is home safely, is she not?" Alana's stare was pointed.

Xander clenched his jaw. "No thanks to myself. My mother rescued us both. It was my father's plan. *I* could not save us."

"Is that what's bothering you? That you couldn't manage alone?" Surprise was stamped all over her pretty face.

"Nay."

Was that it?

Xander was afraid to answer the question.

Alana shook her head. "I will not sit here and argue with you, cousin. I suggest you meet your bride in the chapel at the appointed time. If not, I shall tell my husband to allow his brother to beat you to a pulp for taking her innocence." She arched a delicate eyebrow that dared him to call her bluff.

chapter twenty-two

The longer he remained in his room, the more the walls closed in on Xander. He needed out, needed some air. He mourned his wings, longing to launch into the air, to have the ability to stretch his arms and legs and float, or ride thermals that mussed his hair and cleared his head.

He settled for a long run—he'd been lucky to sneak out of Dunvegan and avoid contact with Duncan or the laird.

Xander had gone far down the beach, stopping when he neared the cave that contained the Faery Stones. He'd reveled in the tingle Alana's *Keep Out* spell shot down his spine. He'd run until his lungs and legs burned, then jumped into the frigid salt water to bathe. The cold ocean had cleansed him more than the run, but his chest—his heart—was still heavy.

He stared hard at the door to his room. If he went back inside, he'd feel just as trapped as he had earlier. Glancing over his shoulder, he thought of Janet in her room, down at the other end of the wide corridor.

Is she crying?

She hadn't even looked at him at supper.

Xander had allowed Alana to block everyone's

thoughts from him magically, because he couldn't cope with *that* as well as his anguish over the woman he loved.

I could go to her.

He shook his head. He placed a shaking hand on the door handle and pushed it open. Shock rolled over him and he forced one foot in front of the other so he could enter the room and close the door.

Janet was sitting on his bed.

Her diaphanous chemise wasn't what made his heart skip. Xander had seen—and tasted—every inch of her gorgeous body before, after all.

She looked up, a small smile on her beautiful face.

His heart skipped.

How could she smile at him after he'd rejected her?

Was she a vision?

A dream?

Xander blinked, but when he opened his eyes, she was still sitting there, as if she belonged in his rooms.

She does belong here.

Hairbrush in hand, Janet made long strokes of her dark locks, spreading them out into a long curtain as she moved her hands. As if she'd sat on his bed every night to brush out tangles as a part of her routine.

He stood about five feet from the end of the bed. Had to swallow hard. He should order her to leave.

Our…wedding is supposed to be in the morning.

If Duncan caught Janet in his rooms, a grave would be more necessary than the priest who was currently in a Dunvegan guestroom.

"Hi," Janet whispered, using the shortened greeting Claire often uttered.

"Hello," he returned, but his voice cracked. Xander wanted to throw the bond open so he could sense what she was feeling.

"We need ta speak."

"As you wish."

Janet put the brush on the table next to his bed and stood, but Xander didn't—couldn't—move.
She came closer but didn't reach for him.

"I want bairns," she blurted. Her cheeks went pink, and she broke eye contact.

The sincerity in her expression made his heart skip.

Maybe Alana was right.

He'd vowed he wouldn't fight the bond, but truth be told, Xander had never *wanted* to fight it. He'd wanted Janet from the start.

The only human mind he couldn't read.

She calmed him. She always had.

He'd crushed her.

Rejected her.

Xander had let his pride push away the woman he loved. He'd been the wounded one—in his own mind. He'd made decisions for her, not allowing Janet to tell him what she was feeling. Afterward, he'd committed the ultimate wrong by rejecting the bond when she'd tried to reopen it.

Alana was right.

I'm a fool.

Janet had come to his rooms, proving yet again she was stronger than he'd ever imagined.

She's reaching out to me.

She's stronger than me.

The earthy scent of peat burning in the large fireplace mixed with the appeal that was just his wife. The aromas tickled Xander's nose and made him want to snatch her to his chest and kiss her.

He owed her an apology first. "I'm sorry."

Those sapphire eyes were wide as saucers as they collided with his gaze. Janet said nothing.

"I was a fool."

She nodded. "Go on."

"When we got captured, I failed to protect you. When I saw—" Xander's voice cracked and he had to clear his throat, "I thought I'd failed you in the worst way a man could fail his wife."

Janet took a step toward him.

He could feel the heat coming off her body and he tried not to stare; he could see her creamy flesh through the thin fabric of her chemise.

"They dinnae hurt me. Yer da stopped it. Ye dinnae fail me. They took yer magic, Xander. They were hurting ye. *Ye* were as helpless as I. Blame dinnae lie with ye."

Xander nodded, because he couldn't speak.

"Both yer parents helped us ta get home, Xander.

That is all tha' matters."

Again, he nodded. His tongue was glued to the roof of his mouth.

"I want ta be with ye," Janet whispered. Her voice was wrapped in honesty, hurt, and hope. "I care abou' nothin' else."

His stomach somersaulted as he stared into her beautiful eyes. He couldn't—*wouldn't*—reject her again. Xander didn't *want* to. "As you wish."

A ghost of a smile played at her delectable mouth. "I do wish it. But do ye?"

"Aye," he whispered.

"As I said, I wish fer wee ones, too."

He smiled, weight lifting off his chest. "Anything in my power, for you. I'm yours."

Her eyebrows knitted together. "I need ye ta want them, too."

Xander had to touch her. He contented himself by caressing her cheek and tucking some flyaway strands of her hair behind her ear. His heart stuttered when his wife leaned into his fingertips. "I do."

Her gaze searched his face. "Truly?"

"Only if they're yours."

Janet's cheeks went crimson, but she nodded. Her lips parted and air rushed from her mouth. When her breasts heaved in her see-through sleeping garment, it took all Xander was made of not to crush her to him and take her mouth, then take her.

He needed her in his arms—in his bed—every

night.

He loved her.

"Janey—"

"I need ye ta love me."

They spoke at the same time.

Her embarrassment was palpable even though the bond was still only an echo in the back of his mind.

She shifted on her feet and broke their eye contact again. Janet stood close, but not close enough.

Xander tamped down his elation and cupped her face. Forced her to meet his eyes. "Done."

She shook her head but didn't pull away from him. "How can ye promise such things?"

"Because." He tried to sound serious but couldn't hold back his grin.

"Because?"

"I already love you."

A whimper fell from her lips even as the first tear rolled down her cheek.

Xander thumbed it away and brushed a kiss to her mouth.

"I love ye, too," Janet whispered.

His pulse pounded in his ears.

They stared at each other.

Neither said a word.

All he could smell was her. The appeal of the peat faded. Xander didn't think of the saccharine scent of the colored woods Fae burned in their hearths or miss them.

Janet was all he could see.

Sense.

Need.

Love.

Heat shot down his spine, spreading slowly over his limbs to settle deep. His cock stirred and tingled as it went from *interested* to *overwhelmed.*

Xander tugged her to him and took her mouth. She kissed him back until they wobbled against each other.

Her perfect breasts were flat against his chest, her lovely hips flush against his.

He ran his hands down her back, the soft linen giving him pause as his palm followed the curve of her bottom.

They had too many clothes on.

"Wait," Janet breathed into his lips.

"What's wrong?" Xander panted, his arousal already throbbing in his trews for her.

"The mating bond. I want it open. I want ta feel ye completely." The words—as well as the desire in her eyes—shot a tremor down his spine as good as a caress.

He nodded. "Take my hands, *mò aingeal.* Call the magic to you, like you did before. I shall do the same and the bond will open. You will feel me, and I shall feel you. Always."

"As it should be." Janet smiled and closed her eyes.

Her beauty stunned him. Xander watched her; the magic made her skin glow. Warmth spread up his arms and across his chest, then continued, down his legs and up his back. Tingling was next, and his cock jerked.

The mating bond solidified and appeared as the golden rope, disappearing into her chest and his.

Janet sighed and opened her eyes, a dreamy smile curving her kiss-swollen lips. "I feel yer heart echoing mine."

"I feel yours, as well."

She nestled close and stood tiptoe to kiss him.

Xander claimed her mouth gently, cupping the back of her neck.

Janet yelped a protest when he pulled back. "What's wrong?"

"You should go to your room."

"Why?" She frowned.

"We are not yet wed."

Janet smirked, and it was adorable. "What 'tis but *one* night? An' besides, we are a Fae mated pair, dinnae?"

Xander chuckled. "Aye, but as your brother said, we are not joined by *MacLeod* standards. If we're to have those bairns you want, I need to keep my bollocks."

Janet giggled and slipped her arms around his neck. "I shall stay here with ye. Duncan, Alex, an' my da dinnae find ou'."

She spread little kisses along his jaw line that sent desire straight to his cock.

The bond's magic hit him with a force that almost

knocked Xander off his feet. He'd grown used to it being muted. Janet's love and passion for him enveloped him and he trembled against her.

"One condition," he forced out.

"What's tha'?" She stared up at him.

"Meet me in the chapel in the morning?"

Janet squealed and threw herself into his arms. "Aye, I've the perfect gown!"

Xander chuckled and kissed her. "I missed our bond, *mò aingeal.*"

"I dinnae like bein' shut out from ye."

"I love you, my strong lass."

"I love ye, my Fae Warrior."

His heart leapt, because her words were echoed, enhanced by the magic that joined them.

Xander helped her out of the lacy chemise, then gathered her up into his arms to place her at the center of his bed. He divested himself of his own clothing, glad he'd rinsed the sweat from his body in the frigid waters.

"Come ta me," Janet whispered, spreading her arms wide as she beckoned.

He settled over her, propping himself above her and caressing her cheek. "I will always. We will always belong to each other. Bound by magic, but also by love."

"Love is more important than magic."

Xander chuckled. "You're right, *mò aingeal.* Thank you for showing me that."

Janet smiled; her sapphire eyes misty. "I ken magic. Now show me love."

He dipped his head down and proceeded to do just that.

The End

about the author

USA Today Bestselling, award winning author of romantic suspense, epic and historical fantasy romance, C.A. loves to dabble in different genres. If it's a good story, she'll write it, no matter where it seems to fit!

She's a hopeless romantic and always will be. Risking it all for Happily Ever After is what she lives by!

C.A. is originally from Ohio, but got to Texas as soon as she could. She's happily married and has a bachelor's degree in Criminal Justice.

She's always writing, and helps small business owners by writing their websites, and she loves it!

WEBSITE: http://www.caszarek.com
EBOOK STORE:

https://www.caszarek.com/ebook-store
PAPERBACK STORE:
https://www.caszarek.com/paperback-store
FACEBOOK:
http://www.facebook.com/caszarek
INSTAGRAM:
https://www.instagram.com/caszarek/
TWITTER: https://twitter.com/caszarek
BOOKBUB:
https://www.bookbub.com/profile/c-a-szarek
GOODREADS:https://www.goodreads.com/author/show/5815085.C_A_Szarek
EMAIL: ca@caszarek.com

You can sign up for C.A.'s newsletter on her website, as well as buy all her books!

www.ingramcontent.com/pod-product-compliance
Lightning Source LLC
Chambersburg PA
CBHW061546210726
48287CB00006B/2092